Brutal Brûlée

Leighann Dobbs

This is a work of fiction.

None of it is real. All names, places, and events are products of the author's imagination. Any resemblance to real names, places, or events are purely coincidental, and should not be construed as being real.

Chapter One

Lexy Baker-Perilla aimed the blue flame at the sugar crystals sitting on the creamy surface of the custard.

Poof.

The flame whooshed out for the third time in a row. Lexy straightened and let out a sigh. She couldn't figure out why the flame wouldn't stay lit. Maybe the ghost of Wellington Manse really *was* blowing it out.

She moved the baking sheet with its rows of custard-filled ramekins away from the window—the more likely cause of the flame going out. The windows and doors in the old mansion weren't very tight and the building was drafty. She probably should have picked a different dessert.

But her grandmother's dear friend, Violet Rutherford, wanted crème brûlée and Lexy was nothing if not accommodating. It was a blessing and a curse—a blessing because her willingness to accommodate her customers had made her bakery very popular, and a curse because she couldn't say no, which was how she'd ended up catering this selective event at Violet's new bed and breakfast in the first place.

Lexy had a special relationship with her grandmother, Mona Baker, whom she referred to as Nans. She'd do anything for Nans. So when Nans asked her to come to the old mansion that Violet had recently purchased to convert into a bed and breakfast, to make the desserts for the weekend, Lexy's accommodating nature had made it impossible to refuse.

It was an easy job that paid well. She didn't have to cook all the food, just make desserts and a few breakfast pastries. It barely took a few hours every day and the rest of the time she got to relax with her homicide detective husband, Jack, and her dog, Sprinkles. The vast estate was nestled in the mountains of Vermont, so they'd had plenty of time to stroll the magnificent gardens and watch Sprinkles zip around on the lush green lawn.

"*Meow!*" Houdini, the house cat, rubbed his face against the corner of the stainless steel freezer—a new addition to the former residential kitchen that Violet had recently had retro-fitted for the more commercial use of a bed and breakfast.

"Shoo." Lexy waved her hands at the jet black cat. Cats had no place in a kitchen and it wouldn't do to have little black hairs in her crème brûlée. Not that Lexy had anything against cats—she liked them well enough, although Sprinkles seemed to have another opinion.

Sprinkles and Houdini had gotten off on the wrong foot when Sprinkles had darted toward the cat during their introduction, sending the cat into a hissing, clawing rage. Lexy thought Sprinkles just wanted to play, but apparently Houdini was not in the mood. Since then, Lexy had tried to make sure Sprinkles kept her distance.

Luckily, they didn't cross paths often, even though sometimes it was unavoidable as the aptly named cat had a habit of appearing out of nowhere like he had done just now. Earlier that day, Lexy had sworn she'd seen the cat at the top of the stairs, only to find him in the conservatory a few minutes later. But such was the way of cats. They were furtive and sneaky—not predictable, like dogs.

Lexy bent over the custard and tried again. This time the flame stayed lit.

"Lovely, lovely!" Violet floated in on a cloud of gardenia-scented lavender and gray chiffon. "That will certainly impress the guests!"

Lexy was warmed by Violet's enthusiasm. She'd been incredibly complimentary of all of the scones Lexy had made for breakfast and tea cakes she'd supplied at noon. Lexy had to admit it was good for her ego, especially since she rarely made crème brûlée which why she'd snuck off into the kitchen to practice her technique in the middle of the

4

afternoon before she had to do it for real after supper.

"Thanks. I just hope it stays lit so I can get through the whole tray." Lexy pointed toward the rows of white ramekins.

"Oh? Is our ghost blowing the flame out?" Violet winked at Lexy. "That might be something to put in the documentary. A real ghost would be good for business."

"Not if it steals people's jewelry," Nans said from the doorway. The two women laughed at Nans' reference to the old story of a ghost haunting the thirty-five room mansion.

According to the tale, a valuable, antique tiara loaded with gemstones had been stolen from a European princess who had been staying at the mansion twenty-five years ago. Neither the thief nor the tiara had ever been recovered. The press had had a field day with the case, dubbing the perpetrator 'The Ghost of Wellington Manse'.

When the owner of the mansion had died mysteriously two months later, it added fuel to the media fire. The publicity eventually died down, but no one wanted to buy the house and it sat abandoned for twenty-five years, then finally went into foreclosure. Violet had purchased it from the bank at a discount due to its dilapidated condition, and she'd been working on restoring it piece by piece.

When Violet had learned that the eccentric producer Leonard Bottaccio was planning on doing a documentary about the ghost legend, she saw her chance for free advertising and invited the production crew to come stay at the mansion even though the renovations were not yet complete. They'd arrived just that morning in a flurry of suitcases and filming equipment.

That's why she wanted Lexy to bring in her special dessert expertise. Violet already had a head chef but hadn't had time to interview dessert chefs yet. She figured it was in her best interest to have everyone raving about the great food they were served during filming, and she wanted the desserts to be top notch.

"There won't be a repeat of that on my watch," Violet said. "I have a new security system being installed as we speak."

Nans' green eyes sparkled. "Really? You can spy on your guests in their rooms?"

"No. That would be crass, Mona." Violet rolled her eyes. "But I can see who is coming and going from the kitchen, library and stairway. No one can get in or out without me knowing."

"Not even a ghost?" Leonard Bottaccio swept in from the screen door that led to the herb garden. He was a tall, thin man in his mid-seventies. He had the energy of a teenager, but dressed like he'd just stepped out of the 1970s. Tonight, he was wearing a navy blue suit with a wide, red and gray striped tie. He held his wrist up and Lexy noticed a line of blood.

Violet grabbed his hand, her forehead creasing as she pushed up his diamond cuff-linked sleeve to reveal four thin lines on his wrist. Lexy watched as angry dots of blood formed along them.

"I was out in the garden looking at your basil and that vile, creature of yours scratched me."

"Houdini?" Violet seemed genuinely perplexed. "Why, he's such a dear, he wouldn't harm a fly. Are you sure it wasn't just a thorn from one of the rose bushes?"

Leonard snorted. "No. Look at the scratches. They match the size of a cats claws."

Lexy looked. They were exactly the right width and distance to match the razor sharp claws of a cat. She turned toward Houdini who blinked a golden eye at her.

"Well, no matter, let me get you fixed up." Violet dragged Leonard over to the sink and turned on the water. "Are you sure the ghost didn't scare him?"

Violet winked at Nans over Leonard's shoulder.

Leonard watched her run his wrist under the water, a gleam forming in his eye. "Now that would be an interesting angle. Cats would certainly see ghosts before people."

"No doubt." Violet twisted around, her eye falling on one of the maids who helped clean rooms and serve meals. "Oh, Karen, can you get me some bandages?"

"Of course." Karen looked around uncertainly. "Where are they?"

"Sorry. I forgot that you're just filling in for Darlene." Violet nodded toward an old, seven-foot tall wooden cabinet decorated with carved gargoyles. "They're in the third drawer of the monstrosity."

"Is that what you call that thing?" Nans asked.

Violet laughed. "Yes. It's very Gothic, isn't it? It came with the place and it's too big to move out. But it comes in handy for storing stuff."

"It sure fits nicely with a ghost legend," Leonard said as Violet applied the bandages that Karen had handed her. "In fact, I think I'll need to work that piece into the documentary."

Lexy looked back at 'the monstrosity' where Karen was familiarizing herself with the contents of the drawers. She wouldn't be surprised to find a picture of it in the dictionary under *Gothic*. Tall, dark wood and heavily carved with gargoyles and north wind faces. It had a certain appeal to it ... if you liked haunted houses, which Leonard obviously did.

"There, now. That should fix you up." Violet patted Leonard's bandaged arm. "Those shouldn't trouble you too much. The scratches were superficial."

Leonard rubbed his wrist and looked around warily for Houdini. "Thanks. I'm sure I'll forget all about them once we sit down to dinner. When is dinner?"

"Seven p.m. Two hours." Violet nodded at a plump, middle-aged woman who was wrestling a stainless steel pot big enough to cook a rhinoceros onto the stove. "Cook is just getting ready to start." She turned Leonard around and led him out of the kitchen. "And you've already gotten a sneak peek at the dessert. Now don't tell anyone …"

Her voice trailed off and Lexy turned back to her torch, switching on the flame and applying it to the top of the custard in even strokes. In the background, she could hear the cook reprimanding Karen in a harsh voice.

Apparently, Karen wasn't much of a fill-in judging by the way the cook was talking to her. Lexy felt sorry for the girl, but she had her own problems with the crème brûlée.

She turned back to her task, hoping that the ghost of Wellington Manse would find something to amuse himself with in another part of the mansion and leave Lexy, and her torch, alone.

Chapter Two

"There's no such thing as ghosts," Ruth whispered later that night at dinner to the six of them seated at a round table in the impressive dining room. The room had recently been renovated and boasted twenty-foot tall ceilings, a limestone fireplace with hand-sculpted cherubs, and four Waterford crystal chandeliers.

White linen-clad tables decorated with real silver, fine china and crystal sat dotted around the room. Lexy was seated with Jack, Nans and Nans' three friends, Ruth, Ida and Helen, to whom Violet had been kind enough to extend an invitation.

Nans leaned toward Ruth. "Don't tell anyone. These guys think ghosts are real."

"I think having a ghost would spice things up," Ida said.

Jack rolled his eyes, focusing on slathering his baked potato with butter.

"It sure would," Helen twittered. "You never know what might happen around here. There could be a mystery to solve right under our noses and a ghost would certainly add an intriguing twist."

Lexy followed Helen's gaze to a small table in the corner where a mustached man sat by himself. The man had been introduced to her as Gustav Schilling and he seemed to be a loner. Leonard had said he was a special consultant hired on for this documentary. Gustav kept to himself and didn't interact with the other crew members.

Lexy figured he was probably just antisocial, but she'd heard Nans, Ruth, Ida and Helen talking about him earlier. They'd found him to be suspicious, which wasn't unusual considering that they fancied themselves to be amateur detectives and were in the habit of thinking of everyone as being suspicious even when no crime had been committed.

The clackity-clack of stilettos on marble signaled the entrance of Gloria Leigh. Lexy looked up from her filet mignon to see the middle-aged former starlet make her entrance. The woman seemed to have an endless supply of stilettos—she'd only arrived that morning and had already worn three different pairs.

The current pair was bright red. Lexy recognized them as Steve Madden's and felt a sudden pang of nostalgia. She used to wear stilettos all the time, too, but had opted for more comfortable footwear over a year ago.

It was one thing to bebop around in stilettos when you were in your twenties, but Lexy was in her thirties now and she needed more practical footwear, especially since she was on her feet all day at the bakery.

She wondered how Gloria managed it. The woman must have been fifteen years Lexy's senior, yet she glided around as if she were walking on clouds. Of course you could hear her coming a mile away with the marble floors that covered every square inch of the mansion, but Lexy was discovering that could be a good thing—especially if you wanted to avoid talking to her.

"Am I late?" Gloria's face was wide with innocence as if she didn't know she was late. She paused in the doorway just under the largest of the chandeliers, her red, glittery dress sparkling as if it had batteries. Lexy got the impression she'd been late and interrupted dinner on purpose so as to be noticed by everyone. Under that innocent veneer, Gloria Leigh knew exactly what she was doing.

Ever the gracious host, Violet cooed, "No, dear. Please just have a seat and I will have Karen bring you something from the kitchen. Tonight we have a choice of filet mignon or Chilean sea bass. Which would you prefer?"

Gloria patted her trim stomach and said, "I'll have to have the sea bass. I'm watching my girlish figure."

Violet nodded to Karen, who scurried off to collect the dinner. A few people rolled their eyes.

Lexy had noticed that happened a lot around Gloria. She was an aging actress who had had a momentary flash of fame twenty years ago, which had died out quickly. Gloria was still kind of a diva, but Leonard had insisted on having her in the documentary because she'd grown up in town and had a connection to Wellington Manse.

"Gloria, dear," Leonard cooed. "Tell us what you know about the ghost of Wellington Manse."

Gloria perched on the edge of her chair, beaming at the attention. "Well, I don't know that much ..." She paused for effect, her wide, blue eyes looking around at everyone at the large head table where she was seated. "But I did think I saw the ghost one night when I was visiting here."

A hush fell over the dining room and everyone strained to hear what she had to say next. Lexy thought Gloria was probably being overly dramatic.

"It was right around the time that Princess Tatiana was staying here. I was sitting in the main hall and I saw a ghostly apparition float down the main stairs."

"What did it look like?" Leonard stared at her with rapt attention.

"You know, all misty and stuff." Gloria waved her hands around. The chunky, jeweled rings she wore sparked off the light of the chandeliers.

Lexy remembered reading something about Gloria having to sell off her jewelry for money years ago. She felt a pang of sympathy for the woman. She was just a fading starlet that needed money. She wondered if Gloria was embellishing for Leonard in order to get more time in front of the camera and if more camera time equated to more pay?

"So, you knew the Wellingtons?" Mrs. Pendrake, a full-bosomed older woman seated across from Gloria asked.

Gloria nodded and started in on her sea bass.

"You must have been here all the time, then." Danny Manning, the associate producer, tapped his knife on the white linen tablecloth annoyingly. Lexy had noticed the man was a bundle of nerves and energy, the type that couldn't sit still.

"Well, not all the time. I did have other places to go to, you know," Gloria answered.

"So, then you lived here in town when the tiara was stolen?" Joy, one of the camera crew, asked.

Gloria nodded. "Yes. I was here then ... I mean not here in the mansion, here in town."

"Do you have any insider information? Like who stole it?" Mrs. Pendrake leaned forward, eager to hear any gossip. Lexy was surprised she didn't already know who stole it as she seemed to be one of those busybodies that knew everything that was going on. Violet had told them that Mrs. Pendrake had found out about the documentary and showed up wanting to stay as a guest. Leonard had persuaded Violet to accommodate her, saying her 'local color' would add depth to the production.

Gloria laughed, but instead of the twitter that Lexy expected, it sounded more like a garbage disposal grating marbles. "Well, it must have been the ghost because no one ever found out who did it."

Leonard clapped his hands. "This is marvelous. I didn't know you'd actually seen the ghost. This will lend an authentic air."

Gloria beamed and batted her eyelashes, obviously pleased with herself and possibly even flirting with him.

Danny nodded enthusiastically. "This'll be great. Just great. A real great addition. It was so smart of you to include Gloria, Leonard." Like any good assistant, Danny sucked up to his boss.

"That's why I make the big bucks," Leonard said.

Danny's mouth flattened into a thin line. Was he jealous that Leonard made so much more than he? He'd mentioned something being 'above his pay scale' earlier in the day, but Lexy hadn't paid much attention to the context. It was really none of her business, anyway.

Lexy noticed everyone was done with their dinner. She leaned over and squeezed Jack's hand, then whispered, "I'm going to get dessert ready."

She slipped out of her seat and headed to the kitchen as unobtrusively as possible. Since she knew exactly how much flame to give the crème brûlée now, it would only take a few minutes and she'd have the perfect dessert.

She pushed the swinging door open to the empty kitchen. Well, not entirely empty. Karen was in there fumbling to disconnect a call on her cell phone, her cheeks deep crimson.

"Oh, sorry," Lexy said.

Karen slipped the phone into her apron pocket and mumbled an apology. Lexy felt a twinge of sympathy for the girl. Violet probably didn't allow personal calls during work hours and Lexy had caught her red-handed.

"Don't worry," Lexy soothed. "What happens in the kitchen, stays in the kitchen."

Karen smiled and scurried out the door, leaving Lexy to her work. The desserts came out perfectly browned and crusted but not burned. Lexy beamed with pride as Karen and two other staff members passed them around.

Everyone oohed and aahed over them, except the mustached man. Lexy noticed he had left even before dessert was served.

When the last person was done dabbing their lips with the crisp white linen napkins, Leonard clapped his hands loudly.

The room fell silent and he stood up. "Everyone, we will start promptly at seven tomorrow morning. I want you all to look lively, so early to bed is recommended." He took a plastic amber pill bottle full to the top out of his pocket and shook it. "I have my sleeping helpers here and, since I'm feeling a little chill, I will take a hot toddy in my room in ten minutes. I suggest the rest of you wind down and retire for the evening as well."

A murmur floated across the room. It was only eight o'clock, but Lexy got the impression that most of the crew was probably used to Leonard's odd schedule.

"Now, now. No complaints. You people are lucky and I know you will want to be well-rested." He paused and surveyed the group. "Because tomorrow I will expose the real secret of Wellington Manse and *you* will all be the first to know it!"

Chapter Three

The next morning, Lexy woke up with the taste of whiskey and lemon on her tongue. Who knew that hot toddies were made out of such vile ingredients? It turned out that Nans was some sort of hot toddy expert and Violet had called upon her to make the drink for Leonard.

Lexy had tried one herself and ended up throwing half of it down the drain, but she still felt sluggish.

Sprinkles, on the other hand, was as peppy as a spring daffodil. Lexy left Jack in bed, wound her brown hair into a ponytail and put the harness on the small, white shitzu-poodle mix, letting the dog drag her halfway down the hall. In front of the library, Sprinkles let out an excited "Yip!" and darted inside, ripping the leash out of Lexy's hand before she could stop her.

"Meow! Hiss!"

Houdini had been napping on the couch. He leaped off, humped his back and swiped at Sprinkles.

"Yipe!"

Sprinkles jumped back and Houdini clawed his way across the top of the couch and up the green velvet drapes. He jumped onto the top of a bookshelf and crouched there, glaring and hissing at Sprinkles.

"Sprinkles, cut it out. The cat does not want to play." Lexy checked Sprinkles for damage and then, not finding any, picked up the end of the leash and shot Houdini an apologetic look.

Lexy dragged Sprinkles out of the room and down the front stairs. Then they went through the conservatory to the grassy area outside where Sprinkles busied herself sniffing an azalea bush.

"*Hiss!*"

A black paw shot out from under the bush.

"*Yipe!*"

Sprinkles jumped back and a black ball of fur shot out of the bush, hurtling around the side of the house out of sight.

"Was that Houdini? How did he get out here so fast?"

Sprinkles whined her answer and Lexy squatted down to inspect the dog again. This time, she had one little scratch. By the way the dog was carrying on, you'd think she'd been mortally wounded, but it was merely a surface scratch.

"You're okay." Lexy patted her between the ears. "You want a treat?"

That perked the dog up and she happily trotted behind Lexy to the terrace where Nans, Ruth, Ida and Helen were seated at a white, wrought-iron table.

"Look who decided to get up." Nans leaned down to scratch Sprinkles behind the ears, then squinted back up at Lexy. "Was that half a hot toddy too much for you?"

Ida snickered, then covered her mouth.

"I guess so." Lexy shot Ida a look. "What time is it?"

"It's seven-thirty," Ruth answered.

"It is?" Lexy could see most of the production crew sitting around the terrace at the tables. Danny Manning paced rapidly back and forth. "What is everyone doing out here? I thought filming started at seven."

"I know, but Leonard hasn't come down yet and everyone is dying to find out the secret," Helen said. Leonard had refused to expound on his announcement the night before despite everyone's begging.

"That's right," Ruth added without looking up from her iPad.

Lexy craned her neck to see what was on the screen. It looked like some kind of plant.

Ruth, who had recently been studying formal gardening, caught her looking. "I'm gathering data on some of the plants in the gardens. They're rather overgrown right now, but Violet plans to set them right. There are some rare varieties here. I'm looking them up on the internet and cataloguing them for her."

"That sounds like fun," Lexy said as Ida rolled her eyes. Gardening wasn't exciting enough for Ida.

"I say we go wake Leonard up," Joy said loudly.

"I agree. We have to get started," a navy T-shirted man from the production crew replied. "Come on, Danny, let's go roust him."

The two of them took off inside and Joy got up from her table, her hand wrapped around a thick mug of coffee. "I'll start getting set up."

"Let's go in and watch," Nans suggested. "I want to find out what his big secret is."

"Oh, good. These chairs hurt my tush," Helen said.

The terrace was filled with the sound of wrought-iron scraping cement as everyone got up and traipsed inside. Lexy was careful to cinch up Sprinkles' leash so as to avoid another altercation with Houdini.

Lexy could hear them knocking on Leonard's bedroom door upstairs.

"Leo. Come on, get up."

"Leo!"

Joy appeared beside Lexy, shuffling uneasily on her feet. "I've never known Leonard to be late." Her voice carried an ominous timber.

Louder knocking came from upstairs. The group had gathered at the bottom of the stairs and a few of them started walking up.

"Just open the door," Danny said.

The sounds of the brass doorknob rattling drifted down the stairs. "It's locked."

"Leo!"

No answer.

By now, the group was at the top of the stairs. They could see Danny and the navy-shirted crew member huddled in front of Leonard's door.

Danny's fingers drummed the side of the door nervously. He turned to face the crowd. "Who has a key?"

Everyone turned to look at Violet, who shook her head. "I don't have any of the keys to this place. They said they'd been lost long ago."

"We're going to have to break in. He could be hurt in there," someone said.

Navy Shirt frowned at the speaker. "What? No, you can't break the door down. It's solid oak."

Jack had been roused by the commotion and stepped forward to inspect the door. He shrugged. "You might be able to crack it loose from the door frame with enough force."

"Leonard. We're all waiting!" Danny yelled.

No answer.

Danny and Navy Shirt looked at each other. "Okay, everyone stand back. We'll have a run at it."

Everyone shuffled back a step, and Danny and the other man rammed their shoulders against the door. Lexy heard the sound of splitting wood but the door didn't cave in.

"Again!" More splitting wood. Lexy could see the fresh wood along the door frame, but not enough for the door to open.

"Again!" This time the door burst open. Lexy could see someone lying in the bed. Danny ran to the bed. "Leo!" Danny shook the figure.

An amber bottle rolled out of Leo's hand and clattered to the floor, then rolled under the bed.

Mrs. Pendrake pushed her way inside the room, waddled to the bed and leaned over. She let out a shriek. "Someone call 911!"

Everyone scrambled for their cell phones as Danny turned a ghostly pale face toward the crowd.

"It's too late. He's already dead."

Chapter Four

"Wait a minute." Jack pushed through to the side of the bed. "I'm a homicide detective. Let me take a look."

"Homicide!" Mrs. Pendrake gasped. "But surely, you don't ..."

"I don't think this is homicide." Jack put his fingertips to Leonard's neck, then pried open an eyelid. "Yep, he's dead. Sorry."

"We still have to call 911," Ida said.

Lexy noticed that Nans had made her way into the room and was looking things over as if it were a crime scene, which Lexy was sure it wasn't—Leonard was an old man and his heart had probably just given out.

Nans studied the way he was positioned in the bed then her eyes swept the room, coming to rest on the hot toddy glass on his nightstand. She bent down, putting her nose near the glass, then straightened. Finally, she bent down to get a closer look at the empty pill bottle under the bed, then came back out to stand with the rest of them in the hall.

Violet had gotten busy on the house phone that sat in a niche a few feet down the hall and was telling the police one of her guests had regrettably 'expired' in his sleep.

"Well, that's a fine how do you do," Ida said. "I guess we'll never know what the big secret was now."

"I'm sure somebody on the film crew knows what it was." Ruth turned to look at the crowd. "Right?"

Everyone shook their heads.

"Leonard liked to keep some of the details of the documentaries under wraps so that the competitors wouldn't find out and scoop us," Joy said.

"Really?" Helen's brows ticked up. "The competition is that fierce?"

Joy nodded and Lexy saw Helen, Nans, Ruth and Ida exchange a look.

"Okay, nobody touch anything. Everybody out of the room while we wait for the police to come." Jack's police training kicked in and he secured the area, even though Lexy was sure it wasn't a crime scene—thus no securing was necessary.

The police arrived in record time. Inspector Garrity was a short, stocky man in his mid-50s with a day's worth of salt-and-pepper stubble on his chin and a full head of matching hair. He wore a brown suit, his shiny police badge clipped to his belt.

He spent some time looking at the body and then turned to Jack.

"Who found him?"

"We all did."

Garrity's brows ticked up. "You *all* did?"

"He was late to start production this morning so we came up to get him," Danny said.

"Production?"

"We're filming a documentary. Leo was the executive producer," Danny said.

"And you are?"

"Assistant producer."

Garrity nodded slowly, sizing Danny up. The sizing up seemed to make Danny more nervous than ever and his lip twitched while his foot tapped spastically.

"Did anyone touch anything?" Garrity asked Jack.

"Just the body and the bed."

Garrity walked to the door and looked at the splintered wood frame. The brass chain lock was still attached. One side had been ripped from the door when they broke in.

"You broke the door down or was it like that?"

"We had to break it down, it was locked. Leo wouldn't answer and we had no other way of getting in," Navy Shirt volunteered.

"There are no keys in this place?" Garrity asked.

Violet spoke up. "No. I don't have keys to the doors, I'm afraid."

Garrity gave one of his slow nods again. "And who was the last person to see the deceased?"

Gloria appeared, floating down the hallway behind them, hugging the wall on the same side as Leonard's room as if she might collapse without its support. She drifted toward them dramatically in her flowing, blue silk bathrobe. She had an embroidered hanky in her hand which she used to dab the corners of her eyes with while she tearfully said, "I think we were all last to see him. He pronounced right after dinner that we should all go to bed early and then left for his room."

"That's right. He was going up to his room and he wanted a hot toddy." Danny was still beside the bed, his leg tapping to some beat only he could hear.

"And his sleeping pills," Nans added, pointing to the bottle under the bed.

Garrity bent down to look, then motioned to a latex-gloved crime scene investigator, who retrieved and bagged the bottle.

"He had these at dinner?" Garrity pointed to the bottle.

"Yes. He always took them to help him sleep," Joy said.

"How full was the bottle?" Garrity asked.

"It was very full," Nans answered.

"The bottle fell out of his hand onto the floor when Danny tried to wake him," Ida added.

Garrity eyed Nans and Ida as if wondering how reliable their old memories were. He looked around the bed table and bedding, then addressed the CSIs. "Search the room for pills. They must have fallen somewhere." He turned to the crowd. "So he went straight to his room and locked himself in and no one else saw him after that."

"That's right," Violet said. "Wait. Not quite. Karen delivered the hot toddy to him."

Garrity addressed the crowd. "Which one of you is Karen?"

"She's not here. She's one of my helpers," Violet said. "She should be down in the kitchen. Do you want me to get her?"

"No, there's no need. This seems pretty cut and dried." Garrity squinted at Violet. "So, you're the owner, Ma'am?"

"Yes."

Garrity turned to Jack. "And who might you be?"

Jack stuck out his hand. "Homicide Detective Jack Perillo from Brook Ridge Falls, at your service."

Garrity shook Jack's hand. "Thanks, but I hardly think I'll need a homicide detective. This looks like an overdose, probably an accident ... or on purpose."

Nans pressed her lips together. "I think you might want to take a closer look at the drink glass."

Garrity spun slowly to look at her. "Who are you? Miss Marple?"

A twitter ruffled through the crowd, but Nans just raised her left brow and patiently watched the inspector who did, indeed, go over to the glass. He bent down and looked into it from the side, then went over to the other side, then looked down from above. Finally, he nodded to one of the many crime scene techs who had invaded the room, and the glass was put in a plastic bag.

Nans remained silent, but her lips ticked up in a satisfied smile.

Garrity threw his arms up in the air. "Okay, everyone out. We need to process the scene. There's nothing to worry about. It looks like this was just a terrible accident, but police procedure dictates that you all stick around and give a statement. I wish these older folks would learn how dangerous it is to mix pills with alcohol." This last sentence he muttered under his breath, then made shooing motions with his hands.

The other police personnel helped push people out of the room and down the hall.

Everyone congregated in the dining room where Violet brought trays of pastries and scones from the kitchen. Two police detectives circulated the room, taking statements from the crew.

Lexy put Sprinkles in their room, then came down and sat with Jack, Nans, Ruth, Ida and Helen. The older women had sparkles in their eyes as they talked about the morning's events.

"I saw you over by that glass, Mona. What do you think was in there?" Ruth asked.

"I don't know. It smelled a little funny, but I'd hate to jump to conclusions."

Jack frowned at Nans. "What do you mean *funny*? You think someone tampered with the drink?"

Nans shrugged. "I don't know."

"I certainly hope not," Ida said. "Because you're the one who made the drink, so you'd be suspect number one."

Karen appeared at Lexy's elbow with a coffee carafe. Lexy watched the shaky stream of brown liquid fill her cup, then splash onto the saucer.

"You seem awfully upset, dear." Ida looked up at Karen.

"It's very upsetting, what happened to Mr. Bottaccio. Was it a heart attack?"

Nans patted her lip with a napkin. "Oh, I should say not. He had his sleeping pills in his hand but the bottle appeared to be empty."

"I distinctly remember that bottle was full last night." Helen unfolded her napkin and put a scone in the middle.

"That's right," Ruth agreed without looking up from her iPad.

"You think he killed himself?" Karen asked incredulously. "He seemed so happy and full of life."

Helen folded the napkin over the scone like a package and shoved it into her giant, tan patent-leather purse. "He may have taken too many pills by accident."

"More coffee over here!" Violet signaled to Karen. She looked upset at the girl, probably because she was spending too much time at Lexy's table and not keeping the coffee cups full. Or maybe she was upset that Leonard's death might scare customers away from the bed and breakfast.

At the table next to them, Lexy could hear some of the crew talking about the fate of the documentary.

"Do you think they will cancel the production?" Joy asked.

"I hope not. We'd be out a couple of days' pay if they sent us home," someone answered.

"But nobody knows what the big twist was."

"Maybe the producers know what it was." The guy in the navy shirt who had helped break the door down twisted in his seat to look at the table behind him. "Danny, do you have any idea what the big secret for the documentary was?"

Danny shook his head. He chugged down his coffee then put the mug on the table, his fingers tapping against the rim while he signaled for another fill-up. Lexy thought the last thing he needed was more caffeine. "I don't know what it was, but I have a call into corporate right now. Hopefully I can take over the executive producer job and we can still do the documentary as planned. If they don't know what Leonard had planned, we can still proceed with the story on the ghost. I think that's compelling enough."

"Maybe Gustav knows," Joy suggested.

Everyone's heads swiveled around, looking for the mustached man, but he was not in the room.

The detectives made their way to Lexy's table and took statements from all six of them. Lexy was surprised that Nans and the ladies answered the questions politely instead of interrogating the detectives like they normally would.

As soon as they were done giving their statements, Garrity appeared in the dining room. He declined Violet's offer of coffee and announced that they were done upstairs for now, but no one was to go in the room until he gave it the all clear. Everyone was to go about their business as usual.

"But what happened? How did he die?" someone asked.

Garrity paused and studied the group. "Well, at first, I suspected he took too many pills by accident. Even in younger people, mixing sleeping pills with alcohol can have some severe effects but in a man of Leonard's age ... well ..." He let his voice trail off.

"What do you mean by 'at first'?" Nans asked.

"Right. That's what I suspected at first but the funny thing is, you said the pill bottle was full at dinner and we haven't found any pills in his room. The pill bottle was empty when it fell out of his hand, so where did the rest of the pills go?"

A murmur ran through the crowd.

Garrity continued. "Leonard's door was locked from the inside. The chain is still attached, so the only logical conclusion is that he took all the pills himself. That would be way too many pills just to help him sleep. I'm sorry to tell you that it looks like Leonard Bottaccio took his own life."

Chapter Five

"Suicide my patootie," Nans said after Garrity and his entourage had made their exit. "That man was full of vim and vigor. Did he seem like a man who would take his own life?"

"Now, ladies, let's not jump to conclusions ... like you *usually* do." Jack slid his eyes over to Nans. "You don't really think one of the people in this room is a killer, do you?"

Nans looked around at the room, her eyes narrowed in suspicion.

"Don't answer that," Jack said. "Let's just leave it to the police."

"Sure. He probably just passed out and the pills fell to the floor and bounced into the crevices. The grout on these floor tiles is loose in some spots. They probably just fell in there." Ida snagged a lone Danish that sat on the plate and wrapped it in a napkin, which she tucked into her purse.

The four ladies pushed up from the table.

"Let's not waste our lovely time here thinking about murder. Let's go outside. I want to show you the rare lady slippers I found growing by the fountain." Ruth tapped her iPad and headed toward the French doors that opened to the garden, with Nans, Ida and Helen close behind her.

Jack covered Lexy's hand with his. "Do you have some free time out of the kitchen?"

Lexy nodded. "I have a few hours before I need to do some prep work. I'm all yours."

Jack raised his left brow suggestively. "Then let's take Sprinkles for a walk in the garden. It's such a beautiful day and we can enjoy some time together."

Sprinkles was in the room, so they went upstairs, walking solemnly by Leonard's room. Lexy cringed at the yellow crime scene tape making a big 'x' in the doorway.

"*Meow!*"

Houdini appeared in the doorway, rubbing his tail in the tape, which had become fuzzy with black fur.

"Stay out of there, Houdini. If there're pills on the floor they could kill you." Lexy peered into the room, a cold feeling spreading in her chest. It felt like a ghost had walked right through her. A ghost? No, that was crazy.

She shooed the cat away and when he was safely in the library, they proceeded to their room, harnessed Sprinkles and went back downstairs, this time taking the back stairway that came out beside the kitchen, where they used the kitchen door to get outside.

"Let's go down here." Jack pointed to where the ground sloped down behind the building. It was overgrown with the most beautiful, vibrant pink roses that provided a striking contrast to the dark stone walls of the mansion.

"*Hiss!*" Houdini darted out at Sprinkles, who had been sniffing a moss-covered bird bath.

"*Woof!*" Sprinkles started after the cat at full speed, then yanked to a quick stop at the end of his leash. "*Yipe!*"

"That cat is everywhere," Jack said as Sprinkles trotted back to them.

"Now, don't go chasing him anymore." Lexy squatted down to pet Sprinkles while she lectured her. "He has sharp claws and you could get hurt."

"This is almost like our own private garden. No one else is down here," Lexy said.

"It's a bit out of the way." Jack looked up at the mansion, which towered four stories above them. "I guess we must be at the basement level. The pond is over there at this level, but then the grass slopes up. You can't see it from here but the terrace must be over on the east side."

"Oh, that's why there're no windows here." Lexy pointed to the stone walls where a few adventurous vines had started to scale toward the upper floors. "I like it down here, it's private."

Lexy took Jack's arm and they sauntered around the garden, enjoying the peace and quiet for almost an hour. They strolled over to the pond which was a bit muddy at the edges. Sprinkles, undaunted by the mud, explored the edges, not caring that the white fur on her paws was turning a reddish brown.

Eventually, they found themselves climbing up the grassy area toward the terrace where Nans, Ruth, Ida and Helen were seated at one of the wrought-iron tables, their heads bent over Ruth's iPad.

"Whatcha up to?" Lexy asked.

"Oh, nothing. Ruth was just showing us the different species of plants she's identified in the garden." Ida rolled her eyes behind Ruth's back.

"Hi, Sprinkles!" Helen bent down to pet the dog, picking up her reddish-stained paw. "You know, a mixture of cornstarch and hydrogen peroxide might take these stains out, Lexy."

"Thanks," Lexy said. She noticed Nans looking absently at the paw Helen held while straining to hear the conversation that Danny and two of the other production crew members were having two tables over. The sound of Danny's voice, pitched high in anger, drifted toward them.

"I deserve that job after putting up with Leonard all these years."

"Shhh..." One of the others at the table mumbled something Lexy couldn't make out. She bent down, pretending she was adjusting something on Sprinkles' harness, and scooted a few inches toward the table.

"I did everything ... won't matter .... the production is better off without him ..." She could only make out snatches of the conversation. She looked up to see Nans adjusting her hearing aid. The sneak was turning it up so she could hear them better.

Clackity. Clack. Clack.

They turned to see Gloria coming up the steps in a short, navy blue skirt and navy and white high heels. With a navy and white striped shirt, she looked like she was ready for a boating expedition.

"What's going on? Are we going to proceed with the documentary?" she squeaked.

Nans jumped at the sound of her voice. Her hand flew to her ear to adjust the hearing aid as she scowled at the former starlet, her eyes drifting down to the hem of the very short skirt.

"Oh, dear, what happened to your leg?" Nans pointed at six red scratches on Gloria's leg.

Gloria glanced down. "Oh. That cat. He scratched me." She adjusted her skirt in an attempt to cover the scratches.

"You should put something on that. Cat scratches can get infected," Helen said.

darted from Jack to Nans. "You two *will* get to the bottom of this, won't you?"

"I hardly think you need us." Jack gestured toward Garrity. "Inspector Garrity seems quite competent."

"Yes, but I don't *know* him and I doubt he'll look out for me like you two will."

Nans patted Violet's arm. "Don't worry, dear, we'll look out for you." She gave Jack 'the look', the one she used to give to Lexy when she was a kid and she wanted Lexy to do something. Apparently it worked on Lexy's husband, too. "Won't we, Jack?"

"Yes," Jack sighed.

Nans was a good amateur detective. She'd even been pulled in to consult on a few cases by Jack and she, Ruth, Ida and Helen had helped him solve more than one crime.

"Shh..!" Mrs. Pendrake leaned over from the next table to shush them. "The inspector is talking."

Garrity *was* still talking. "... We'll need to reconstruct the night's events so I want everyone to think about if they saw anything strange or unusual. Did anyone see anything outside Mr. Bottaccio's room? Or anything at all suspicious?"

"You think one of *us* is the killer?" someone asked.

"One or more."

The crowd erupted in angry whispers.

Helen scanned the terrace. "Maybe the killer will make a break for it."

"Maybe he already did," Ida said. "I don't see that mustache guy here."

"Oh, no, he's not the killer. He's a nice man," Ruth cut in. "I talked to him out by the irises and he knows a lot about flowers."

Nans eyes slid over to Ruth. "Just because he likes flowers doesn't mean he's not the killer, Ruth."

"Shh.." Mrs. Pendrake looked at them sharply.

Garrity was *still* talking. "We'll need to go over the timeline in more detail than we did this morning. Who saw Mr. Bottaccio last?"

"We all did, at dinner," Danny said. "Remember he told us all to go to bed early."

Garrity cocked his head to the side and squinted. "No, that wasn't the last time anyone saw him because he had a drink brought to his room, didn't he?"

"That was *her*," someone pointed out and everyone looked over to where Karen was fumbling a tray of dishes and mugs. One mug slid off and shattered on the floor.

"Umm... Hi," Karen looked at Garrity meekly. "That *was* me. I brought him a drink."

"Okay, then I'll start my questioning with you," Garrity said.

The crowd quieted down as Karen walked off with Garrity and then everyone started whispering.

Violet's hand flew to her chest. "You don't think it was Karen? Why would she kill Leonard? She didn't even know the man."

"He's just talking to her. That doesn't mean he suspects her," Jack said. "She was the last person to be seen with Leonard and she brought him the drink, which I assume must have had the poison in it. He's just starting with her because it's the logical place to start."

Nans' eyes narrowed. "I did notice that the girl doesn't seem to have very good waitressing skills. You said she was temporary help, didn't you, Violet?"

"Yes, that's right. She's filling in for my regular girl Darlene. Darlene had to go out of town for her grandfather's funeral and she recommended Karen. In retrospect, I should have just gone to the agency and gotten someone temporarily, but Darlene assured me Karen could do the job."

Lexy remembered how she'd caught Karen making that phone call in the kitchen. Karen had seemed upset that she'd been caught. Lexy wondered if she was upset because Violet didn't like people taking calls during working hours, or perhaps there was a more sinister reason.

Behind them, a chair scraped on the cement as Mrs. Pendrake scooted her chair closer to their table. "I couldn't help but overhear. Did you say that Darlene was out of town for her grandfather's funeral?"

"Yes, that's right," Violet said. "She went to California and will be back on Monday. Do you know her?"

Mrs. Pendrake nodded. "Oh, yes. Darlene Cross, right?"

"Yes."

"Hmmm." Mrs. Pendrake's gray eyebrows tugged together and her lips pursed into a thin line. "Well, that's very strange because I took a trip into town for a new blouse this morning and I saw Darlene at *Ellerton's Fashions* ... and she was buying a mighty expensive outfit."

Chapter Seven

Lexy could practically see fireworks going off in Nans' eyes when Mrs. Pendrake mentioned that Darlene was still in town. She knew her grandmother smelled something fishy and would want to investigate. But Lexy had to get in the kitchen and start cooking, so Nans got Darlene's address from Violet and she Ruth, Ida and Helen borrowed Violet's car to see if they could talk to Darlene. Luckily, she lived right in town, so they weren't disobeying Garrity's orders.

Jack went to talk to Garrity to see if he could wrangle any inside information out of him. Lexy headed to the kitchen where she gathered the ingredients to make magic bars for dessert. She'd already planned on double chocolate cake and red velvet cake with vanilla frosting but, by the way the way things were going already, she had a feeling they might need lots of desserts by the time the day was over.

Three hours later, Lexy had finished in the kitchen and Nans and the ladies were back and bursting with excitement. Violet ushered them into the conservatory and shut the French doors so they could talk without being overheard.

Nans, Ida and Helen sat on one of the white wicker sofas. Ruth walked over to the window, inspecting the plants. Lexy stood next to the fireplace.

"What did you find out?" Violet asked anxiously. "Was she really in town?"

"Yes, I'm afraid so," Nans said.

"But why would she lie to me?"

"The age-old reason. Money."

"Money usually does it," Ruth said as she fingered the leaves of a ficus.

Violet started pacing. "I don't understand why Darlene would lie. Did Karen need the money from the job that badly?"

"No, it's not that. Karen *paid* her to get this position here."

"Why?"

"That's a good question," Ida said. "Darlene didn't know the answer, but Karen paid her an awful lot of money, so it must have been pretty important for her to insinuate herself in this house."

Violet sucked in a breath. "Then she must be the killer!"

Nans lips twisted. "It would seem that way. But then, the question is ... what was her motive?"

"I think she was up to something. Yesterday, in the kitchen, I saw her being very secretive about a phone call. I thought maybe she just didn't want to get caught making a personal call on work time, but maybe it was something else," Lexy said.

Violet nodded. "I've never made a rule about that. Most of the help has the common sense not to carry their phones around when they're working."

"*Meow!*" Houdini mashed his face up against the outside of one of the French doors that led to the lower garden.

"My word, that cat is everywhere!" Ruth walked over to let him in, stopping at a potted plant whose sickly brown leaves were drooping to the floor. "This peace lily could use some care."

Once inside, Houdini ran over to Violet who scooped him up in her arms, petting him soothingly.

Back at the window, Ruth fussed with the plant. She was really getting into this gardening thing, thought Lexy. Nans glanced over at her, a frown creasing her forehead. Maybe Nans didn't like the way Ruth's new obsession with plants was distracting her from their amateur detecting activities.

"Any-whoo," Ida broke into everyone's thoughts, clearly eager to get on with the investigation. "It sounds like this Karen is suspect numero uno."

"I wonder if Garrity knows?" Helen asked.

"That should be easy enough to find out." Nans tilted her chin toward the door that led to the hallway, and Lexy saw Jack and Inspector Garrity walking toward them.

Violet dropped Houdini, who landed on the floor with a soft thud and a belligerent meow, then she opened the door for Jack and Garrity. "What is it inspector Garrity? Have you carted Karen off to jail?"

"No."

"Why ever not?"

"No reason to put her in jail."

Nans frowned at Garrity. "We heard she might have some questionable motives."

Garrity looked at Jack. "You were right. They were investigating. Do they do this all the time?"

Jack shrugged. "Yep. I'm sorry to tell you there's no stopping them, you might as well just join forces with them."

Garrity nodded slowly as he considered it. "Okay. I'll bite. You tell me what you know and I'll tell you what I know."

Ruth, Ida and Helen exchanged a look. Each gave a slight nod to Nans, who then described their visit with Darlene and how she'd admitted that Karen had paid her to make up a story so Karen could replace her at the mansion.

Garrity listened intently nodding his head. "Well that corroborates what she told me."

"So, she *is* the killer?" Violet sank into one of the wicker cushioned chairs, her hand fluttered around her neck. "Oh dear, I hired a killer."

"I didn't say that," Garrity said. "I said the story of her paying Darlene corroborates what Karen told me."

A look of confusion crossed Helen's face. "She's not the killer?"

Garrity shook his head. "I don't think so. She *did* pay Darlene to get this job here. But it actually wasn't for her. It was for the management of the production company that is doing this documentary."

"Why would they do that?" Nans asked.

"It seems there's a mole in the company. Someone is passing along the documentary ideas to a rival production company. Apparently, good ideas are worth a lot of money. But they don't know who it is, so upper management hired Karen to infiltrate and see if she could ferret out the mole."

"And that's why she paid off Darlene?" Violet asked.

"Yep. The company gave Karen the money to pay Darlene, and Darlene persuaded you to hire her."

"Are you sure she's not just making that up, you know, so you'll let her go and she can make a getaway?" Ida asked.

Garrity's face twisted comically. "Gee, I didn't think of that." He paused then leveled Ida with a look. "Naturally we made a phone call and checked it out. She's legit. But I'd appreciate it if you ladies didn't tell anyone. It's in our best interest to keep that secret while the investigation is on-going. If the killer thinks we suspect Karen, he might get sloppy and screw up."

"That's why she was being so secretive on the phone and why she didn't really have any relevant experience," Lexy said.

"That's right."

"And you don't have any other clues or suspects?" Nans asked.

"The pill bottle was wiped clean, so there were no prints on it. We never found the extra pills. We figure the killer either disposed of them or still has them. The hot toddy was laced with cyanide." Garrity's eyes twinkled as he turned to Nans. "You made the hot toddy so, you might be my next suspect."

Nans bristled. "I hardly think I would have a motive."

"That's the problem. We don't know who *did* have a motive."

"Wait a minute," Lexy said. "You said that Karen was here to look for a mole in the production

51

company. Someone who's giving secrets to a rival company."

"That's right."

"If there is a mole, then maybe Leonard caught him or her and threatened to prosecute. That might be a motive for murder."

Garrity twisted his lips together. "Possibly. Leonard's room was locked from the inside which means he must have let the killer in. Once inside, the killer probably distracted him and added the cyanide to his glass. We need to find out who he let into the room last night."

"Too bad no one has come forward to say they saw someone," Lexy said.

Nans tapped her fingers on her lips. "Maybe somebody saw something and they just don't realize it's important."

"Like that busybody Mrs. Pendrake. She seems to be everywhere," Helen leaned back to look out into the hallway as if expending Mrs. Pendrake to be out there spying on them. "She probably saw something."

"Maybe, but is she reliable?" Ruth asked.

"Are any of them?" Ida replied.

Nans snapped her fingers. "We don't need Mrs. Pendrake or any other witness. I think we have something much more reliable."

"Whats that?" Jack asked.

Nans turned to Violet. "Didn't you say you'd installed a security system that would show anyone entering the library?"

"Yes, I have valuable books in there."

"Well, Leonard's room was right next to the library."

Violet shot out of her seat. "That's right! Leonard was in the blue room. The camera is pointed at the hallway outside that room. Whoever went in there last night would be captured on the computer files."

Chapter Eight

They rushed over to the other side of the mansion where Violet had her office in a small room off the kitchen. The room had once been some sort of sitting room, Lexy guessed, but now it was retrofitted with a large oak desk facing out a set of double windows that looked out onto the herb garden.

Violet slid behind the desk and they all crowded around her. She pecked at the keys with one finger in a maddeningly slow pace as she searched for the security program.

"Here it is." She hovered the cursor over an icon and clicked it with a flourish. A screen came up and she stared at it with her lips pressed together. "Now, how do I get the access to the data from last night?"

Ruth, who was a computer whiz, had been leaning over Violet's shoulder. "Let me try." She pushed Violet out of the way and sat down at the keys, her fingers flying over them. A few seconds later, they were looking at a picture of the upstairs hallway. The view was directed at the library but just on the edge of the screen you could see the door to the room Leonard had been staying in. The door was shut.

"*Mew!*" Houdini jumped on the desk, situated himself in front of the monitor, blocking everyone's view, and then blinked at them as if they were all looking in his direction to admire him instead of just trying to see the screen he was now blocking.

"Out of the way." Ruth pushed him to the side. He lashed his tail in the air, hitting Ruth in the face before turning in a figure eight and settling in front of the screen again.

Violet picked him up and deposited him on the floor. "Shoo, Houdini, we have important business here."

They heard footsteps in the hall and Garrity looked out. "Oh, Karen, please come in here. I want you to see this. We know you went to Leonard's room last night. Maybe something on this tape will jog your memory."

Karen crowded in the room behind them. "What is that?"

"It's the security system," Violet said.

"I didn't know you had one."

"I don't think anyone does. Hopefully, that'll work in our favor," Jack said. "Because the killer might not know there was one, either. We're trying to see who went into Leonard's room last night."

As they watched, a small dark figure appeared at the bottom of the screen. Houdini. He trotted down the hallway and disappeared into the library.

55

"Is this time-stamped?" Garrity asked.

"Yes, it's tied into the computer clock." Violet pointed to tiny numbers on the bottom right of the screen.

"Maybe we should fast forward it," Ida muttered impatiently. "Otherwise, we might be here all day."

"We don't have to. It's motion activated so we'll only see when there's activity and then it shuts off after five minutes," Violet said.

"What are you guys doing?" They turned and saw the guy with the navy shirt who had helped Danny break into Leonard's room. They were attracting quite a crowd, but Garrity didn't seem to mind. Maybe he wanted people to know they were looking at the security tape, thinking it might push the killer into doing something that would expose him, wondered Lexy.

"We're looking at the security tape of the hallway outside Leonard's room from last night," Jack answered.

"Oh. You're thinking you might see the killer, right?"

Garrity turned and studied the man. "That's right. Do you know anything about what we might see?"

"Not me." He leaned casually against the door frame.

"There's someone!" Nans tapped the screen and we watched Karen come into view. She was holding a tray with two drinks on it. She tapped on Leonard's door. The door cracked open and she handed him the drink, then he shut the door. She turned and walked back in the direction of the stairs.

"As you can see, he was very much alive when I gave him the drink," Karen said. "And I didn't enter his room so I couldn't have messed with the pills."

"You had two drinks on the tray," Helen said. "Who was the other one for?"

"That one was for Gloria. A martini. She wanted it delivered in the conservatory," Karen answered. "I went straight there after I delivered Leonard's drink."

Mrs. Pendrake appeared in the doorway, craning her neck to see what they were doing.

Another person appeared on the screen and Violet gasped. "Isn't that Danny, the associate producer?"

Lexy felt a trill of excitement, but Danny walked past Leonard's room without even a glance.

After a few more minutes of empty hallway, Lexy and Jack appeared with Sprinkles. As they got to the doorway heading into the library, Sprinkles tugged at the leash, setting Lexy off balance. Lexy planted her feet on the ground to hold Sprinkles back while the dog tugged and pulled. It looked comical.

Helen laughed. "What was that all about?"

"Oh, Sprinkles likes to chase Houdini. He was in the library and she tried to have a go at him. I had to hold her back."

"Sprinkles would be wise to keep her distance," Violet said. "Houdini won't hesitate to scratch anything that threatens him and his claws are very sharp."

They continued to watch the monitor intently. The next person was Gustav Schilling, the man with the mustache. He was walking toward the stairs—away from his room—but he, too, walked straight past Leonard's room.

A few more minutes went by, and then they saw Danny again. This time, he was walking toward the stairs. He looked freshly showered and in different clothes from when they had previously seen him.

"This is the next morning," Jack tapped the numbers on the bottom of the screen.

Violet's brows shot up to her hairline. "But that's impossible. We didn't see anyone go into Leo's room after Karen gave him the drink."

"I know," Jack said.

"Well, if no one went into his room, and it was chained from the inside, then who poisoned him and staged it as a suicide by taking his pills?" Nans asked.

A sharp intake of breath came from the back of the crowd. Lexy turned to see Mrs. Pendrake's pale face staring at them. "Glory be! There's only one explanation. It must have been the ghost of Wellington Manse."

Chapter Nine

"That wasn't quite what I was thinking." Nans frowned at Mrs. Pendrake.

"But if it wasn't the ghost, then how did the door get chained? You can't do that from the outside," Helen pointed out.

Nans leaned toward Helen and whispered in a low voice, "This place is loaded with film crew people. They must be savvy about technology. Maybe someone doctored the video."

Jack overheard them. "That's an idea." He turned to Violet. "Who can get into this office?"

"Nearly anyone during the day. At night, it's locked up." Violet pointed to a shiny lock on the top of the door. "I had to have a new lock installed as the original key had gone missing with the rest of them."

"There's another solution, too," Ida said. "Maybe someone switched the pill bottle after dinner. After he shook it around and everyone saw it was full, they could have pickpocketed it and replaced it with a container that had no pills."

"But don't you think Leonard would have noticed that all his pills were gone when he got to his room?" Helen asked.

"He was old. Maybe he forgot how many pills he had or thought he had the wrong bottle." Ida slid her eyes toward Helen. "I know Helen here has several bottles in various states of fullness for her gout.

"Ida!"Helen swiped at Ida's arm and Ida grimaced, but her eyes twinkled mischievously.

"I don't know," Nans said. "How would the killer have known he would even show us the pills? Then he would have to have had another bottle with Leonard's prescription information on it handy to make the switch at the right time. I think the pills being gone was just an added bonus for the killer."

"But if we do take the pill bottle out of the equation, this whole thing makes more sense. We'd only have to figure out how he got the drink with the poison and that would be a lot easier." Jack's eyes slid toward Karen.

Karen pointed at Nans. "Don't look at me. She made the drink. I just delivered it."

"You could have doctored it on the way to his room," Ida suggested.

Karen gestured toward the computer. "Can't you look on that thing? You'll see I didn't put anything in the drink."

"Actually, we can," Violet said. "I remember that Mona and I walked with Karen to the bottom of the stairs. So we know she didn't put anything in it then. The surveillance system monitors the stairs and the hallway to Leonard's room, so we should be able to see if she did anything on the way to his room."

Ruth found the file and they all watched Karen climb the steps and deliver the drink. She was in the clear.

"Did you see anyone else around after you delivered the drink?"

Karen shook her head. "No. Well, other than Gloria because I delivered her a drink in the conservatory. After that, I went back to the kitchen and cleaned up."

Ida let out a disappointed sigh. "So what now? We just sit around and wait for the killer to trip up?"

Nans shook her head. "No, we don't sit still. Next, we look for a motive."

They heard sounds in the hallway and looked over to see Danny Manning walking by, his head bowed, apparently deep in thought. When he noticed the crowd, he stopped and looked at them. "What are you guys doing in here?"

Navy Shirt answered him. "It turns out there is a video surveillance that shows the hallway outside of Leonard's room. We're looking to see who went into his room last night."

Danny's left brow rose a fraction of an inch. "Oh, really? Who was that?"

"That's the thing," Mrs. Pendrake said excitedly. "No one entered Leonard's room. No human, that is.

Which leaves only one answer—it was the ghost of Wellington Manse."

A look of excitement spread on Danny's face. "Really? You guys think Leonard was killed by the ghost?"

He didn't wait for an answer. He'd already pulled his cell phone out and was punching in numbers. As it rang, he turned back to them. "This is perfect! It makes the documentary much more interesting. I'm sure the home office will give us the green light to go ahead now!" He walked off down the hallway with a spring in his step.

Helen and Ida raised their brows at each other and Ida said what both of them were thinking, "That sounds like motive to me."

Chapter Ten

Lexy and the ladies were heading toward the library to go over the clues in private when they heard the familiar clackity-clack-clack of stilettos behind them.

"I saw you all in Violet's office," Gloria said. "What was going on in there? Does Inspector Garrity have any new clues?"

"We were going over the surveillance video," Ruth said.

"Surveillance?" Gloria looked at them with blank eyes.

"Violet has a security system installed and one of the cameras happens to point to the hallway outside the room Leonard was staying in."

Gloria looked toward the ceiling as if she were searching for a camera. "I didn't know there were cameras everywhere."

"They aren't everywhere. Just the hallway and stairs, as far as I know," Ruth said.

"We thought we would see the killer on the video," Ida added.

Gloria's perfectly plucked brows shot up. "And did you?"

Nans shook her head. "Unfortunately, no."

"So who do they think did it?" Gloria shifted on her feet. Lexy didn't blame her for trying to take the weight off. Those stilettos looked mighty uncomfortable.

"We don't know." Nans' face turned thoughtful. "Karen said she brought you a drink in the conservatory. Is that right?"

"Yes. A martini."

"And who were you with in there?"

Gloria laughed. "Nobody? Unless you count the cat."

"How long did you stay there?" Nans persisted.

"Oh, about an hour."

"And did you see anyone else walk by in the hallway or outside?"

Gloria pressed her bright red lips together, the wheels behind her eyes turning slowly. "No."

"What did you do after?"

She shrugged. "I went to bed." Then her eyes widened. "Oh! But I did see someone on the way to bed."

They leaned forward with excitement. "Really? Who?"

"Danny Manning. I was crossing the front foyer when something up in the hallway caught my eye. I leaned back to look up through the spindles. It was Danny." She put her index finger to her pouty red lips, her forehead wrinkled in concentration. "He was going to Leo's room and he looked around behind him as if looking for someone or to see if anyone was watching, but he didn't see me because I was down below."

Nans had been listening with rapt attention. "And then what happened?"

She shrugged. "Nothing. I continued on to the back stairs."

"Back stairs?" Ida asked.

"Yes. I spent a lot of time here in my younger days and I know the mansion inside and out. My room is on the opposite side of the hall from Leo's at the back. So, I just take the back stairs. I know Violet doesn't like guests to take them, but I like them better since they seem less formal."

"I take those sometimes," Lexy said. "They come out near the kitchen."

"That's right." Gloria's brow furrowed. "I wonder what Danny was doing at Leo's door."

"Maybe killing him?" Ida suggested.

Gloria's eyes widened. "You don't think so, do you? I probably should've said something before. Do you think it's important?"

"Umm ... yeah," Helen said.

"Maybe I should tell that nice inspector Garrity." Just as Gloria said that, Garrity appeared behind them. "Oh, there he is! Yoo hoo, Inspector."

66

Gloria clip-clopped off toward Garrity and Ida rubbed her hands together.

"It looks like the case is solved. Danny wanted the executive producer job, so he faked Leonard's suicide and doctored the tapes. The added bonus is the ghost angle, which will ensure the production company wants to continue the documentary with him as executive producer."

Nans made a face. "Maybe, but I wonder about the motive. Was that job worth killing over? Plus, he didn't seem at all nervous when we mentioned we were looking at the videos that would show whoever went to Leonard's room."

"That's probably because he knew he'd doctored the tape," Helen suggested.

Nans turned to Ruth. "Is there any way to tell on the computer if someone doctored those tapes?"

"I might be able to tell by looking at the timestamps." Ruth shrugged. "It's kind of a crap shoot, but I could look."

"We should add that to our to-do list. I'm starting to think the motive might have had more to do with the secret Leonard was going to tell than Danny's ambition to be executive producer," Nans said.

"What about the mole?" Ida asked. "He could be the killer."

"That, too," Nans agreed. "Which is why we need to talk to the mysterious mustache man—Gustav Schilling."

Chapter Eleven

Ruth waved her hands in the air. "Pshaw. It couldn't be Gustav. He's a flower-lover. I've talked to him in the garden a few times and he's very nice."

Ruth's face was flushed and Lexy wondered how friendly she was getting with the guy.

"Gustav was seen in the surveillance video walking toward the stairs, which means he was leaving or going downstairs for something," Nans pointed out. "We need to find out where he was going and if he saw someone."

"What do you think, that he went outside and scaled the side of the building to climb through Leonard's window and kill him?" Ruth asked sarcastically.

"Not exactly ... but maybe something close," Nans answered.

They all frowned at her.

"What do you mean?" Ida asked.

"I have a theory. But I'll fill you all in later." Nans turned to Ruth. "Where do you think we can find Gustav?"

"How should I know?" Ruth's voice had a sharp edge, then she said a bit more softly, "Probably in the garden."

"Let's go through the conservatory," Ida suggested. "We can take the French doors to the garden. It's a shortcut."

They headed in that direction, passing the familiar black shape of Houdini skulking down the side of the hallway.

Lexy stopped and bent down to pet his silky fur. "That reminds me, we'd better make this short. I need to take Sprinkles out."

"*Meow!*" Houdini looked at Lexy suspiciously.

"No. Sprinkles isn't here now," Lexy assured the cat as she continued petting him. "Too bad you can't talk, Houdini. I bet you could tell us what happened to Leonard."

Nans nodded. "No doubt. I think Houdini knows a lot more than the rest of us."

"*Meow!*"

Lexy stood up and Houdini trotted off in the opposite direction, bidding them adieu with a flick of his fluffy, black tail. The five of them continued to the conservatory where they found Gustav bending over the sick peace lily that Ruth had pointed out to Violet earlier.

He started when they came in the room. His gaze rested on Ruth, a smile twitching at the corner of his lips. He dipped his chin at them. "Ladies."

"*Meow!*" Houdini raced out of the room.

Lexy's brows mashed together. "What the heck? He was just out in the hallway. Did you guys see that?"

"Yes." Ida stared after the cat. "He's sneaky. Skulking around and seeming to appear out of nowhere. But that's the way with cats, isn't it?"

"Yeah, I guess so," Lexy said. She didn't really know much about cats. She was a dog person and Sprinkles was about all she could handle.

Ruth had made her way over to Gustav.

"What do you think is wrong with it?" Ruth asked, gesturing toward the plant.

"I don't know. Violet told me to come in and look at it, but there seems to be no hope, I'm afraid." He straightened up. "Well, I'll let you ladies enjoy the room."

He started to go out the door to the garden, but Nans stopped him. "Actually, we came here to talk to you."

He turned back to look at them, his brow creased. "Oh? What about?"

"We heard you were here as some sort of consultant to the documentary."

Gustav nodded. "Yes, that's true."

"Can you tell us what it was about?" Nans asked.

A smile broke out underneath Gustav's mustache. "I'm sorry, but I cannot. It's a secret. A surprise."

"Does it have anything to do with the secret Leonard mentioned at dinner last night before he was killed?" Ida asked.

Gustav shrugged. "Maybe. I'm not privy to what Leonard had in mind. I just know why I'm here. I get my orders from the home office."

"Well, you might want to come clean with us," Ida said. "Leonard was murdered and we're looking for the murderer."

Gustav bristled and glanced at Ruth. "Surely, you don't think I had something to do with that."

Nans shrugged. "Probably not, but we did just review the surveillance tapes from last night and we saw you leaving the building late into the night."

"What are you implying? I never went to Leo's room."

"We know you didn't," Ruth soothed, shooting an angry glare at Nans. "But you *were* heading for the front stairs. We were wondering where you went and if you saw anyone."

Gustav relaxed. "Oh. Well, if you must know, it was a full moon and I was going out to the moonlight garden."

Nans scrunched up her face. "Moonlight garden?"

"Yes. It's a type of garden planted especially for viewing in the moonlight. It consists of all white flowers. The one here has peonies, roses and lilacs.

The white flowers seem to glow in the moonlight. It's quite beautiful." He turned to Ruth. "The moon will still be bright tonight. Would you like to come out and see it with me?"

Ruth blushed. "I'd love to," she tittered.

Ida rolled her eyes. "Okay, Romeo, so let me get this straight. You're here on some secret assignment you won't tell us about. You went out in the middle of the night to look at flowers and you didn't see anyone in your travels. Is that right?"

"I never said I didn't see anyone," Gustav said.

"So you did see someone then?" Nans asked.

Gustav's brows tugged together. "I did. They were coming from the lower garden, which was odd because it was very late at night and it's quite dark down there. I couldn't make out exactly who it was but ..." His voice trailed off.

"But you have an idea of who it was, don't you?" Nans asked.

"I do. I would hate to say who I thought it was and be wrong, though. That being said, there's not really another person here that fits the description."

"Well, who was it?" Ida asked impatiently. "There's a killer on the loose and we need to get to the bottom of this."

Gustav shifted uncomfortably. He glanced at Ruth, who gave an encouraging nod. "I can't say for sure and I wouldn't swear to it in a court of law, but it looked an awful lot like Mrs. Pendrake."

Chapter Twelve

They found Mrs. Pendrake in the breakfast room that the production crew was using as a temporary home base for their equipment.

Lexy wasn't surprised to see her snooping around. The woman seemed to be an unabashed busybody.

"Hello, there!" Mrs. Pendrake slid her reading glasses off. They fell to rest on her ample bosom, held there by a chain around her neck. "I was just curious about all this production equipment. It's a whole new world to me. Very interesting." She picked up a pamphlet and handed it to Nans. "Here's their dossier on the subject."

Lexy looked over Nans' shoulder. The pamphlet looked like a copy of old newspaper articles on the twenty-five-year-old legend. One of them had a picture of the tiara, loaded with chunky gemstones.

Mrs. Pendrake leaned her wide hips against the desk and crossed her ankles. Her lemon yellow polyester pants rode up to reveal white socks and white tennis shoes. While her outfit was sharp and well put together, her socks were dingy gray and her shoes stained reddish-brown at the tips. "That was quite a revelation on the surveillance tapes."

"I'm not sure about it being a revelation, but it sure was interesting," Ida said.

Mrs. Pendrake studied Ida. "You don't believe in ghosts?"

Ida shrugged. "I haven't seen any concrete evidence of them so far."

"Well, who else could have killed Mr. Bottaccio?"

"That's what we're trying to find out," Helen said.

Mrs. Pendrake gave them a quizzical look. "Oh, and you think I can help with that?"

"We're not sure," Nans said slyly. "We were wondering if you saw anyone out and about on the grounds last night."

Mrs. Pendrake looked taken aback. "What do you mean? I went to bed right after dinner last night."

"You did?" Ida looked at her sideways. "You weren't outside in the garden?

"No."

Nans' lips twisted. "Did you see anyone in the house? Anyone near Leonard's room?"

Mrs. Pendrake shook her head. "No. Apparently I didn't warrant one of the finer rooms upstairs. Mine is on the first floor. I wouldn't have been able to see anyone coming and going from Leonard's room at all."

"You live in town here, don't you?" Nans asked.

"Yes, I do. I was lucky enough to get a reservation to stay here since Leonard thought I would add some local color to the documentary. It was quite an honor." Mrs. Pendrake's face turned thoughtful. "That poor man. I do hope he didn't suffer."

"He probably didn't," Nans said matter-of-factly. "If you live in town, you must have known Gloria Leigh."

"Well, I knew *of* her. When she was younger. Obviously, she wouldn't remember an old lady like me." Mrs. Pendrake leaned toward them and lowered her voice. "She was kind of a wild thing. No one was surprised when she went off to be an actress. She liked to put on airs back then, and I see she still does."

"What do you mean by that?"

"Well, I hate to gossip, but at dinner she made it sound like she hung around with the Wellingtons, when I believe it was more their servants she hung around with. They were a bit of a rough crowd."

"Oh, I see," Nans said. Mrs. Pendrake was obviously happy to be gossiping despite the fact that she said she hated to gossip. Lexy knew Nans was encouraging her. You never knew what kind of good information you could get out of a gossip.

"Well, she always did like money, even as a little girl. Of course, she got famous but I hear her spending was a lot more than she earned."

"Oh, you don't say?" Ida said. "I heard she had to sell off a lot of her jewelry."

77

"Yes. She likes to wear fine clothes, nice jewelry and those awful shoes." Mrs. Pendrake rolled her eyes. "Who could walk around in those things all day?"

"I used to have shoes like that," Ida said enviously. "I can't wear them now because of my bunions. That girl had better watch out or she's going to end up with feet like mine."

"She sure does seem to have a lot of pairs of them," Lexy said. "These floors are solid stone. Her feet must be killing her, not to mention the constant clack clack noise must drive her crazy."

"I know it's driving me crazy," Ida added.

"And she seems to wear them all the time," Helen said. "I've never seen her with tennis shoes or sandals."

Mrs. Pendrake narrowed her eyes. "Not all the time. Last night I came to the conservatory and the red stilettos were sitting right there next to the rubber tree. I could hardly say I blame the girl. I'm sure her feet were sore."

"So you didn't see or hear anything last night?" Nans asked.

"Nope."

"And you went right to bed after dinner and stayed in your room?"

"Yep."

The four ladies exchanged a glance.

"Okay, well thanks for the help." Nans turned and they all started out of the room.

"You're welcome, though I'm afraid I wasn't very helpful. I just hope you catch the killer. Whether it was a ghost or a human, I fear it's not safe around here."

They left the breakfast room and headed toward the foyer. Nans glanced at the pamphlet in her hand, then her eyes went to the ceiling and stayed there as they walked down the hall.

"Well, that was enlightening, wasn't it?" Ida said.

"What do you mean?" Helen asked. "She said she didn't see anything?"

"Yeah and she said she didn't leave her room or go outside," Ida whispered.

Nans, who had still been staring up at the ceiling, stopped short. "Yes, she did. I'll double check with Violet, but I don't see any surveillance cameras down here, so we have no way of verifying whether she left her room or not."

"That's right," Ida added. "Which means either Gustav was mistaken as to who he saw ... or one of them is lying."

Chapter Thirteen

They parted ways at the front stairs. Nans and the ladies were going out to the terrace and Lexy intended to take Sprinkles for a walk. She texted Jack on the way up the stairs, hoping he could join them.

In the upstairs hall, a crowd had gathered in front of Danny Manning's room. Jack stood outside the door in the hall along with the navy-shirted guy and Joy from the production crew. Gloria stood off to the side.

"What's going on?" Lexy peered inside the room where Garrity and a red-faced Danny were having words.

"I tell you, those are not mine." Danny pointed to a plastic bag that Garrity was holding. Inside the bag, Lexy could make out the pills from the amber pill bottle.

"Garrity did a search of the rooms and he found that in Danny's underwear drawer," Jack filled Lexy in.

"A search? Wouldn't he need a search warrant?" Lexy asked.

"Not if everyone gave him permission. Which they did."

"I'm going to have to take you down to the station, Danny. I have some more questions now that we've found these pills in your room, and a witness says they saw you going in to Leonard's room last night," Garrity said.

"But ... but," Danny sputtered, waving his hands in frustration. "Someone must have put them here. Maybe we can look on that video monitor and see."

Violet had come down the hall and was standing behind Lexy. "I'm afraid that won't work. The cameras only go as far as the library and this room is further down the hall."

Garrity lifted an eyebrow suspiciously. "But you probably already knew that, so that you could try to make like you were set up."

Danny held his hands up. "No. I swear. I *was* set up. You guys know I didn't go into Leo's room. We saw it on the surveillance tape." He turned a pleading face toward Jack, Lexy and Violet.

"We think the killer altered the video to exclude the part where he went to Leonard's room." Garrity led a protesting Danny out of the room and down the hall. "A lot of the evidence points to you, but don't worry. We'll do a thorough investigation and if you really are innocent it will come out," Garrity added as they disappeared down the stairs.

"Well, I guess that's it then!" Violet seemed chipper. "Now we can all get back to business."

In contrast to Violet's happiness, Joy looked down in the dumps. "I don't know what this means for the documentary. There's no producer now, so I guess we need to all start packing our bags."

Navy Shirt spoke up. "Don't be too sure. The company may still let us put it on. Plus, Danny hasn't been *charged* with anything and the inspector didn't say we could leave, so I'm not sure if we can."

"This is certainly interesting. I wonder what Nans will make of it." Lexy whipped out her cell phone and texted Nans.

"I'm sure she'll have something to say." Jack's face looked hard, as if he were deep in thought.

"What do *you* think about it?" Lexy asked.

He pressed his lips together and shook his head. "I'm not convinced it was Danny, though he does have a decent motive."

"Nans said she didn't think the motive of getting the executive producer job was strong enough."

"Oh, he might have had more than just *that* as a motive," Gloria said from behind them.

Lexy turned around, her brows raised in question. "Really? Like what?"

Gloria shrugged. "Oh I don't know. I got the impression maybe Leo had found out something about Danny that he didn't like."

Jack narrowed his eyes at Gloria. "What exactly would that be?"

Gloria blinked at them. "I don't know, exactly. I just got that *impression*. I can't say for sure what it was, although I did hear there might be someone not quite loyal to the group."

Gloria then turned and sashayed away from them. Lexy looked at Jack. "You think Danny could be the mole?"

"Anything's possible."

They proceeded to their room where Sprinkles was anxiously waiting. Lexy gave her a few treats and put her in her harness, the whole time wondering if Danny had been the mole. "You know, Danny would have had the perfect opportunity to go to Leonard's room and the knowledge to doctor the surveillance video. Having worked as Leonard's assistant producer, he'd know what kind of pills Leonard took and might have even picked them up at the pharmacy for him. *And* he'd be the perfect candidate for the rival company to have as their mole, because he'd have the most information about their projects."

"Good points." Jack opened their door and gestured for Lexy and Sprinkles to precede him into the hallway. "If he is the mole, I assume Garrity will find a large deposit of money in his bank account. We'll know soon enough."

They headed downstairs and ran into Nans, Ida and Helen in the foyer.

"Are you off for a walk?" Nans bent down to pet Sprinkles behind the ears.

"We are." Jack leveled a look at Nans. "And what are you up to? Now that the killer's been caught, you must have some extra time on your hands."

Nans waved her hands. "Not at all. I'm still investigating. Garrity can't seriously think it was Danny, can he?"

"Well, a lot of the evidence points to him and he did have the pills in his room," Jack pointed out.

"Fiddlesticks. Those were planted."

"When would someone have done that?" Jack asked.

"Probably the morning we were busy discovering Leonard's body," Ida offered.

"And besides, how do you propose Danny got into Leonard's room to switch the pills?" Nans asked.

"I assume he doctored the video tape as you suggested earlier. He had the skill set."

Nans shook her head. "Nope. Ruth checked that out just a little while ago and those video surveillance tapes were not doctored." Nans looked around. "Where is Ruth, anyway?"

Jack stared at Nans. "That's impossible, because if they weren't doctored then no one went into Leonard's room."

"They weren't doctored," Nans said with certainty.

Jack laughed. "Surely you don't expect me to believe the ghost of Wellington Manse killed Leonard?"

Nans winked. "Maybe. You'll have to wait and see. I'm certain Garrity is making a big mistake, though, because I know who did it and why."

Jack flapped his arms. "If you know all that, then why don't you just tell us?"

Nans' face turned thoughtful. "Because unfortunately I don't know exactly *how* they did it. But once I do, I *will* prove to you exactly who the killer is and I can assure you, it is not Danny Manning."

Chapter Fourteen

The five of them walked out the expansive, double oak doors at the front of the mansion.

"Where do you think Ruth has gotten off to?" Nans asked.

"Probably the garden," Ida answered.

They stopped at the top of the limestone steps. "Well, I guess we'll go that way to look for her." Nans pointed to the right, then turned to Lexy. "Which way are you going?"

"I think over toward the—"

"*Hiss!*"

"*Woof!*"

Houdini had appeared on the steps and Sprinkles lunged for the cat, who humped his back, took a swipe at Sprinkles and then ran inside the mansion just as the front door swung shut. Sprinkles ripped the leash out of Lexy's hand but, since the door was now closed, her efforts to follow the cat inside were thwarted. She raced down the steps in a blur of white fur and ran in a big circle on the front lawn, her leash trailing behind her.

"Sprinkles!" Lexy took off after the dog.

Sprinkles didn't want to be caught. She looked back over her shoulder at Lexy while she picked up speed and darted around the side of the house. Lexy ran after her with Jack close behind. Nans, Ida and Helen followed them, keeping pace with a speed that belied their age.

Lexy followed Sprinkles to the remote garden that she and Jack had visited earlier in the day. This time, there was another visitor there—Ruth. She was bent over, examining the bright pink roses that covered the garden.

Sprinkles stopped short next to Ruth, who bent down to pet the dog.

"*Hiss!*" Houdini's black paw shot out from behind a rosebush, leaving two bloody lines across Sprinkles' nose.

"*Yipe!*" Sprinkles backed off and crouched under another bush, whimpering.

Lexy's heart crunched at the sound of her dog in pain. "Aww, Sprinkles, I told you not to chase that cat."

Lexy bent down to inspect the damage. Her arm scraped against the thorny rose bush. "Ouch!" She drew back, looking at the half-dozen scratches on her arm.

Ruth looked over her shoulder. "You're lucky none of those are bleeding. These roses have very sharp thorns."

"Hey, wait just a minute there," Ida said. "How did that darn cat get down here? I distinctly saw him run into the house and the front door shut behind him. It's almost like there're two of the darn things."

Nans looked at Ida sharply. "That's a good point." She bent to inspect the rosebushes, moving through them to the side of the building.

"Now be careful, Mona," Ruth said. "These roses are very thorny. I've just discovered this is an incredibly rare variety and I think—"

Nans snapped her fingers, interrupting Ruth. "I've got it!"

She pressed her palm against the mansion, looking upward at the expanse of large granite stones. A smile played across her lips as her hand traced the stones of the building. She nodded her head. "Yes, indeed."

She snapped her head around and looked at Jack. "Call Inspector Garrity and have him gather everyone in the conservatory in one hour. I know who the killer is, how they did it and why."

Chapter Fifteen

Nans paced back and forth in front of the stone fireplace, playing it up for the audience in the conservatory, which consisted of everyone involved with the documentary, Violet, Lexy, Jack, Ruth, Ida and Helen. Even Danny Manning was there, having been questioned by Garrity and then released after Ruth proved the videos were not doctored. Garrity seemed to have a lot of faith in the ladies' detecting skills and Lexy figured that was largely due to Jack's vouching for them.

Lexy stood next to a prehistoric-looking potted plant with gigantic leaves. A smile played across her lips as she watched her grandmother pacing back and forth. Lexy figured this was more for effect than anything. Nans, who looked deep in thought, was probably thinking about how to best lay out the clues to her 'audience'.

The room was full of anxious silence. Everyone was on the edge of their seat waiting to hear what Nans had to say. Lexy studied the people in the room. One of them was a killer, but which one? If the guilty person was present, she couldn't tell by the look on his face.

Across the room, she noticed Gustav standing awfully close to Ruth. She hoped he wasn't the killer because it was obvious Ruth had taken a liking to him.

Garrity came in and the crowd stirred.

"Hi, everybody." He leaned against the wall next to Jack, then turned to Nans. "Okay, Columbo, tell us what you got."

Nans clapped her hands together and everyone riveted their attention on her. "Thank you all for coming. As you know, there was a murder here last night. A very cleverly planned murder. A murder made to look like suicide. But the killer screwed up a few details ... and that killer is in this room with us right now."

A nervous murmur rippled through the crowd.

Garrity rolled his eyes and whispered to Jack, "Is she always this dramatic?"

Nans fixed him with a glare. "Quiet, please."

"Wait a minute," Mrs. Pendrake spoke up. "I thought Danny Manning was the killer." She pointed to Danny who was standing over by the glass doors that led to the garden. "He had the pills in his room and he had a motive."

"Ahh." Nans held her index finger up. "That's what the killer *wanted* you to think. Those pills were obviously planted. I knew right away Danny couldn't be the killer because no one would be so stupid as to keep the pills in their room to be found as evidence later on. He would have simply flushed them down the toilet."

"What about Karen? Didn't she make the drink that killed him?" Joy asked.

"Yes, I had my sights on Karen, too. But video surveillance proved she did not doctor the drink. Though our investigation did turn up the fact that she's not quite who she seems to be."

"What does that mean?" someone asked.

"Although Karen isn't the killer, she *was* sent here for a specific purpose: to ferret out another questionable person—the mole."

One of the guys from the production crew screwed his face up. "Mole? What mole?"

"There's a mole in this group. Someone who is spying on the project so that they could bring the information to a rival production company. Karen was hired by your corporate headquarters to find out who that person was."

People shifted in their seats and looked at each other suspiciously.

"And that person killed Leo?" someone asked.

"At one point I thought so, but I think you'll see as I lay out the clues that the mole and the killer were two separate people."

"Just get on with that, lady. *Who* is the killer?"

Nans gave the heckler a sharp look. "I will reveal the killer in due time. But first, I want to lay out exactly what led to their discovery."

Nans glanced over at Garrity who made a circular 'move-it-along' motion with his hand.

She continued. "At first I was quite perplexed as to how someone could have gotten into Leonard's room. We thought the video had been altered. Any one of you would have the skill set to do that." Nans paused and looked over the production crew who were, again, glancing around at each other.

"But, my colleague, Ruth," Nans gestured toward Ruth, "is somewhat of a computer expert and she deemed the files had not been tampered with. So we knew some trickery must be going on."

"I think it was him!" Joy stabbed a finger in the direction of Gustav Schilling, who seemed nonplussed by her accusation.

Nans nodded. "At first, I suspected him, as well. He was even seen on the surveillance tape mysteriously going outside in the middle of the night. When we questioned him, he tried to cast suspicion on someone else, claiming to have seen them outside, but when we questioned that person, they denied being out there."

"So we knew one of them was lying," Ida chimed in, earning a 'look' from Nans. Apparently, Nans didn't like sharing the limelight with anyone, not even Ida.

"Yes, someone was lying. But who?" Nans paused for effect then turned sharply in the direction of Mrs. Pendrake.

"Mrs. Pendrake, you said you went right to bed after dinner, but I think that was a lie. It was you out in the garden that Gustav saw, wasn't it?"

Mrs. Pendrake's hands fluttered at her neck as her cheeks turned red. "Well, I never. Are you calling me a liar?"

Ida twisted in her seat to look at Mrs. Pendrake. "Yes."

Mrs. Pendrake scowled at Ida.

"I know you *did* lie and I can prove it," Nans said. "And I know why, too."

Mrs. Pendrake bristled. "Really? I don't see how."

Nans pointed to Mrs. Pendrake's shoes. "You have red mud stains on your shoes. That red mud is only located by the Koi pond."

"So? I went to the Koi pond. So what?"

"Yes, but *when* did you go to the Koi pond? That is the question. You couldn't have gone this morning because you told us that you were shopping and you'd seen Darlene in town. When we saw you in the breakfast room, the mud was dry, so, given that you were shopping in the morning and the mud wouldn't have had time to dry if you'd been to the pond after that, you must have visited it before the crack of dawn. My bet is that it was much earlier, like in the middle of the night. Mr. Schilling told the truth. He did see you. You *were* out there last night and you *did* lie to us about that earlier, didn't you?

"This is outrageous! Surely you don't think that I'm the killer?" Mrs. Pendrake's eyes darted from Garrity to Nans.

Nans held her palm up. "No, actually I don't think that you're the killer. *But* I think you *saw* someone when you were out there and you couldn't tell us because you couldn't admit that you were outside in the middle of the night."

Mrs. Pendrake became indignant. "Honestly, these accusations are getting tedious. Why would I not tell you about being outside at night?"

"Because you were outside in a secret rendezvous, passing along information ... Mrs. Pendrake, *you* are the mole!"

The crowd gasped and everyone twisted to look at a crimson-cheeked Mrs. Pendrake.

"Fine. I might have entered into an agreement with a rival company but I didn't mean anyone any harm. And I certainly didn't kill Mr. Bottaccio. I'm just a naturally curious person and I knew I could find something out. These sorts of things keep me from being bored. At my age, one has to find things to do," she shrugged then her eyes widened. "Wait a minute. I did see someone when I was out there. Do you mean that the killer is—"

"Wait!" Nans cut her off. "Let me continue and see if we have the facts right lest we condemn an innocent person."

Nans' gaze drifted over the room. "I had the hardest time figuring out the motive and it was actually you, Mrs Pendrake who helped me with that."

"Me?" Lexy noticed Mrs. Pendrake was edging toward the door. The angry glares of the production crew must have been getting to her and she was probably trying to secure her departure ahead of an angry mob.

"Yes. When we saw you going through the production crew's things in the breakfast room, the pamphlet you had gave me the clue as to the motive. But I still didn't know how the killer pulled off having the door locked from the inside … until later that day."

"*Meow!*" Houdini appeared at Nans' feet. He wound figure eights around her ankles, purring loudly.

Nans looked down at him and smiled. "In the end, it was Houdini who actually cracked the case."

"The cat?" Navy Shirt looked over at Garrity. "Is she for real? That sounds crazy."

Garrity smiled. "Let's just give her a chance and see where she's going with this."

Nans nodded at Garrity. "You see, when Leonard made the announcement at dinner about revealing the secret of Wellington Manse, the killer must have been afraid that Leonard was going to spill the beans about something that would incriminate them. The killer knew Leonard had to be silenced and came up with a plan to make it look like Leonard had taken too many pills. We'd all seen the full pill bottle in his hand at dinner, right?"

Everyone nodded.

"The killer was very clever, setting it up so it looked like an open and shut case, hoping the police would think that it was suicide or maybe Leonard just got confused and had taken too many pills. With the door locked from the inside, how could they expect foul play?"

"I guess they didn't count on us being here," Ida said proudly.

"No, indeed," Nans said. "Anyway, in order to pull it off, the killer needed to know something about this house. Something that even the new owner, Violet, herself didn't know."

Violet's brows shot up in surprise. Apparently, she wasn't privy to what Nans was about to reveal.

Nans continued, "It wasn't until I saw Houdini in the rose garden that I realized what it was that the killer knew."

"What is it? What does Houdini have to do with this?" Violet asked.

"Did you ever notice that Houdini seems to appear somewhere that he couldn't possibly be?" Nans asked.

"Yes, I did notice that. It's uncanny."

"I thought there were two cats," Joy said. "Is that it?"

Nans shook her head. "No. There is only one Houdini, but he knows a secret and so does the killer."

Nans paused, letting the anticipation build as everyone inched forward in their seats, waiting.

"What is it?" someone finally asked.

"This house has secret passageways." Nans smiled at the looks on the faces of her audience. "That's how Houdini appears to be in two places at once and *that's* how the killer got in and out of Leonard's room without being seen."

A murmur rippled through the crowd.

"Secret passageways? Where?" Violet wanted to know.

"I'll show you after, though I don't know all of them. But I do know the one the killer used. It leads right into the room Leonard was in."

"Oh, dear," Violet said. "That's why we never saw anyone on the tape."

"No one else knew about these passageways?" Navy Shirt turned to look at the rest of the crew, who all shook their heads.

"That's right," Nans said. "No one knew. Not even Violet. She bought the mansion from the bank, and no one at the bank had even been in the house for more than a cursory glance, so they didn't know about them. The renovations haven't gotten far enough to expose any of them, yet. This house has been vacant for twenty-five years, after the previous owner died mysteriously ... of course, now in light of what I've discovered the police might need to open an investigation into his death. Anyway, the only people left alive who would know about the passages are people who lived in or were associated with the house long ago."

"I still don't get it," Joy said. "What was this secret and why was it worth killing over?"

"The killer committed a crime many years ago which has gone unsolved to this day," Nans said.

"You mean the tiara robbery?"

"That's right. The tiara was not stolen by any ghost. It was stolen by Leonard's killer, who used the secret passages to pull off the crime. That person is someone who knows this house inside and out. Someone who spent a lot of time here. And there's only one person here who grew up hanging around in this house."

Nans looked directly at Gloria.

"Who, me? I don't know anything." She back stepped a little toward the French doors leading to the garden.

"I think you do. Last night at dinner, you said you spent a lot of time in this house when you were younger. And the clues prove it. Here's what I think happened." Nans resumed pacing, ticking off the items on her fingers. "After Leonard made the announcement, everyone went their separate ways. Most people went to bed as Leonard suggested. But you stayed in the conservatory and had Karen bring you a drink, thus providing you with an alibi of sorts.

"You didn't stay in the conservatory to drink it, though. You poured the drink out in the plant so when Karen came back later to get the glass, it would look like you had been in here sipping it for quite some time." Nans pointed to the dead peace lily that Ruth had fretted over earlier.

"That's what killed the plant!" Ruth glared at Gloria. "A lovely, innocent plant like that. It's a darn shame."

Nans continued on, ignoring Ruth's outburst, "Then you slipped outside to the lower garden where there's a secret entrance tunnel through the basement. I discovered it earlier today when Sprinkles had an altercation with Houdini.

"I couldn't figure out how the cat could have gotten outside when he had clearly run inside and the door shut behind him minutes before. But when I looked at the stones, I noticed an interesting crack. It was too symmetrical to be the settling of the building and when I looked closer, I could feel air flowing through it. Later on, I went down and verified my suspicions. It was, indeed, an entrance into a secret passageway that runs throughout Wellington Manse."

"So? So what if I put my drink in the plant. Maybe I didn't like the drink anymore. You can't prove I went outside." Gloria's stilettos made sharp little clacks as she shuffled backward toward the door.

"Oh, but I think I can. You left your shoes in the conservatory because you didn't want the clack clack clacking of them to make noise in the passageway. People would have heard you behind the walls. Mrs. Pendrake saw your shoes in here. She told us so herself, didn't you?" Everyone looked at Mrs. Pendrake, who nodded.

"So I took my shoes off? Big deal. My tootsies hurt. I've never even been out to that garden." Gloria had backed right up against the door, her hand behind her back, feeling for the knob.

"You've never been to the garden? Then how did you get those scratches on your leg?" Nans pointed to the six deep scratches on Gloria's thigh.

Gloria looked down. "I told you, the cat scratched me."

"I don't think so. The cat only has *four* claws but you have *six* scratches. Those scratches came from the rose bushes right outside the secret passageway, the ones you had to push through to get to the passage." Nans looked around the room triumphantly. "And there's one final nail in your coffin." Nans turned to Mrs. Pendrake. "You *did* see a person when you were coming back from the Koi pond last night, didn't you?"

Mrs. Pendrake nodded, apparently glad the focus had moved from her being the mole to Gloria being the killer. "Yes, that's right. I saw Gloria and she was coming up from the rose garden."

All eyes were on Gloria as she twisted the doorknob behind her, unlatching the door. She pivoted on her sharp, pointed stiletto heel and lurched out the doorway. Too bad she didn't notice Houdini who had been weaving around her ankles.

Her stiletto pierced his tail.

"*Meowl!*"

He let out a wail that would raise the dead, causing Gloria to mis-step. Her heel broke off. Her foot slammed to the ground sideways, causing her ankle to roll. She stumbled forward and fell right into the arms of the two policemen who had been waiting for her outside.

Chapter Sixteen

"I guess Gloria making a run for it is almost as good as a confession," Ida said to Garrity after the two policemen had carted Gloria away, kicking and screaming.

"Well, that and the fact that she's probably wearing one of the gemstones from the tiara right now," Nans added.

"She is?" Violet walked beside Nans, who was leading everyone down to the garden so she could show them the secret passage.

"Oh, yes. When I saw the pamphlet that Mrs. Pendrake had with the tiara, I recognize the shape of the chunky gemstones as being the same as in some of Gloria's rings," Nans said.

"I remember reading that she had sold off her jewelry periodically over the years," Lexy added.

"That's right," Nans said. "I think she'd been systematically prying the gems out of the tiara and putting them in new pieces of jewelry which she sold off little by little. Inspector Garrity will have an expert inspect them to prove it, of course."

"Gloria might never have been caught if Nans didn't have such a keen eye and Mrs. Pendrake wasn't such a busybody," Jack said.

Lexy glanced behind them. "What happened to Mrs. Pendrake, anyway? She's not with us."

"I suspect she's busy packing her bags. Being the mole, she didn't make any friends here and will probably want to leave as quickly as she can," Nans said.

"Shouldn't she be arrested or something?" Danny asked.

"Technically, she hasn't broken any laws, so there's nothing to arrest her for," Garrity said.

"I'd really like to thank you for finding the killer." Danny reached over to shake hands with Nans as they stopped in front of the rose bushes. "For a while there, I thought it was going to jail for something I didn't do."

Nans nodded. "Gloria must have seen you as the perfect scapegoat and tried to frame you by saying she saw you outside Leonard's door and putting the pills in your room. I think she did it when we were discovering Leonard's body because we would have all been too busy to notice her. I'm not sure whether there's a passageway that opens to the room you're in, or if she simply slipped into your room through the door when we weren't looking.

"She must have come *out* of your room, though, because I remember her making a dramatic show of hugging the wall as if she couldn't make it down the hallway on her own. The wall she was hugging was on the same side of the hallway as your room and Leonard's, but if she had come out of her own room and was hugging the wall she would been on the opposite side of the hall because that's where her room was."

"And she also tried to plant a seed of suspicion by saying that Leonard suspected you of something," Ida added.

"Suspected me of something? What?" Danny asked.

"She wouldn't elaborate on that. But I wasn't fooled by her, anyway," Nans said, stopping in front of the pink roses. "And here we are." She pushed her way carefully through the bushes to the side of the mansion.

Violet followed Nans through the bushes, her gaze set on the large stones. "There's a secret passage in there?"

Nans put her palm out on the surface of the building pushing and pressing, feeling her way around. "Yes, there is, but I'm not sure exactly how ... oh, there it is!" Nans pressed and a stone slid aside revealing a dark, five-inch narrow opening.

"*Meow!*" Houdini trotted inside as if it were second nature to him.

Lexy's brows tugged together as she watched the cat disappear into the darkness. "Wait a minute. I can see how Houdini gets in when you open the door for him but how does he do that on his own?"

"And not only that, but how does the door close behind him?" Joy asked. "If he really is using these passages, there'd be open doors all over the mansion."

"I wondered that too, but watch." Nans called Houdini and he came trotting back outside. A second later the door shut behind him as if by magic. "These passageways have a special spring-triggered mechanism. It's quite ingenious. Once someone slips through the doorway it closes on its own a few seconds later. Houdini inadvertently triggers the doors by rubbing against them in the right place. I don't know how often he uses these passages but he must be quite adept at it by now and it's fascinating he's been able to do it without any of us seeing the openings. Not to mention that the openings are very narrow and strategically placed to blend in with the rooms. One might not even notice a secret panel open at all."

"I would have been pretty freaked out if all of a sudden a secret passage into my room slid open," Navy Shirt said.

"Imagine how Leonard felt when his slid open and Gloria popped into his room," Joyce added.

Danny laughed. "Leonard did like women. He probably thought it was a miracle."

"Yes. Too bad she poisoned his drink," Helen added.

"She must have distracted him, somehow," Ida wiggled her eyebrows, "and then slipped poison into the hot toddy."

"Then she either waited there until he succumbed and positioned him with the empty pill bottle, or came back later," Garrity added.

"And she's the one who stole the tiara twenty-five years ago?" Violet asked.

"And possibly the one who killed Mr. Wellington. If he figured out she'd used the passageways to steal the tiara, she might've had to come back later and do him in. Of course, she probably had an accomplice back then, but we don't know who that was. We suspect it may have been one of the servants whom she was friendly with." Garrity pressed his lips together. "We'll get to the bottom of that, too."

Danny stepped over to the wall, pressing and pushing where he'd seen Nans pressing. He hit the right spot and the stone slid open. "This is fantastic! So, let me see if I have this right. Twenty-five years ago, Gloria used these passages to steal the tiara. That started the whole legend of the ghost of Wellington Manse, right?"

Nans nodded.

Danny whipped his cell phone out of his pocket and turned to the other members of the production crew. "This is even better than the original documentary! When I call the home office and tell them that we've solved the case of the ghost of Wellington Manse and discovered who stole the tiara, I'm certain they'll want us to continue ... they might even want us to step up the production schedule. I need to check these passages out, though. We'll be doing some of the filming in there." He put the phone to his ear and stepped into the passage, the door sliding shut behind him.

"I hope he knows how to get out of there," Ida said.

Joy laughed. "I'm sure he'll figure it out. This whole thing is so sad. Leonard loved his little secrets but keeping the secret about the passageways and the ghost is what got him killed."

"I don't think he suspected that Gloria stole the tiara," Nans said. "Otherwise, he probably wouldn't have hired her on. I think he just found out about the secret passages and suspected that was the way the robbery had been pulled off."

"Actually, he didn't even suspect that much," Gustav, who had been inspecting one of the Rose bushes, said.

"What do you mean?" Helen asked.

"The secret he was going to reveal had nothing to do with the tiara or secret passages," Gustave said.

Lexy's brow furrowed. "Really? Then why was he killed?"

"Oh, I'm sure *Gloria* thought that was the secret and she killed him like you all said, but that's not why Leonard hired me as the expert and, as far as I know, he had no idea about the secret passages."

"Well, then, why did he hire you?" Ida asked. "I thought you were a historian or ghost expert."

"Nope." Gustav pointed to the pink roses. "I'm a horticulturist—a flower expert. These roses here are a very rare species. It seems the original owner of this mansion planted the flowers here over a hundred years ago. They're usually difficult to grow, but for some reason they flourished in this environment. Probably due to certain minerals in the soil. That was the secret Leonard was going to reveal ... rare and valuable roses."

"Oh, for crying out loud," Violet said. "So, Leonard was killed for nothing?"

"Well, not exactly nothing," Nans said. "If he wasn't killed we would have never investigated and we would not have solved the mystery of the ghost of Wellington Manse."

"That's true," Violet looked thoughtful. "And now that the mystery has been solved and these intriguing passageways have been uncovered, I think that's going to be very good for business."

They started walking back toward the conservatory. Lexy and Jack trailed behind Nans, Ida, Helen and Violet. Ruth and Gustav lingered back at the roses.

"You know, I'm looking forward to seeing them film this documentary with this new twist, but after that things are going to seem pretty dull back in Brook Ridge Falls. Don't you think so, Mona?" Ida asked.

"Dull? I should say not. After I write my press release about how we solved the case of the ghost of Wellington Manse, our phones will be flooded with requests for us to solve so many interesting cases we won't have a moment of peace." Nans picked up the pace as they walked up the hill toward the mansion. "So, you girls better rest up now, because once we get home we're going to be busy!"

The end.

***

Want to read about more of Lexy's and Nans' adventures? Get the rest of the Lexy Baker series for your Kindle:

Save 30% when you buy the Lexy Baker Cozy Mystery Boxed Set:

Lexy Baker Cozy Mystery Series Boxed Set Vol 1 (Books 1-4)

Or buy the books separately:

Killer Cupcakes (Book 1)
Dying For Danish (Book 2)
Murder, Money and Marzipan (Book 3)
3 Bodies and a Biscotti (Book 4)
Brownies, Bodies & Bad Guys (Book 5)
Bake, Battle & Roll (Book 6)
Wedded Blintz (Book 7)
Scones, Skulls & Scams (Book 8)
Ice Cream Murder (Book 9)
Mummified Meringues (Book 10)

Sign up for my newsletter and get my books at the lowest discount price:

http://www.leighanndobbs.com/newsletter

If you want to receive a text message on your cell phone when I have a new release, text COZYMYSTERY to 88202 (sorry, this only works for US cell phones!)

A Note From The Author

Thanks so much for reading, *"Brutal Brûlée"*. I hope you liked reading it as much as I loved writing it. If you did, and feel inclined to leave a review, I really would appreciate it.

This is book eleven of the USA Today best selling Lexy Baker series. I plan to write many more books with Lexy, Nans and the gang. I have several other series that I write, too - you can find out more about them on my website http:// www.leighanndobbs.com.

This book has been through many edits with several people and even some software programs, but since nothing is infallible (even the software programs), you might catch a spelling error or mistake and, if you do, I sure would appreciate it if you let me know - you can contact me at: lee@leighanndobbs.com.

Oh, and I love to connect with my readers, so please do visit me on facebook at http:// www.facebook.com/leighanndobbsbooks

Signup to get my newest releases at a discount: http://www.leighanndobbs.com/newsletter

If you want to receive a text message on your cell phone when I have a new release, text COZYMYSTERY to 88202 (sorry, this only works for US cell phones!)

Recipes

Crème Brûlée

Ingredients:

2 1/2 cups heavy cream
6 egg yolks
1 vanilla bean, split and scraped
6 tablespoons white sugar
2 tablespoons brown sugar

Preparation:

Preheat oven to 325 degrees (f).

In a medium saucepan, combine cream and vanilla bean and bring to a boil, stirring constantly. Remove from heat and let sit for 15 minutes.

Beat egg yolks and 4 tablespoons of white sugar until creamy.

Add the cream mixture to the egg yolks a little at a time.

Pour the mixture into ramekins (about 6 8 oz. ramekins) or a small dish. Set the ramekins or dish into a larger baking pan and fill that pan with enough water to reach halfway up the sides of the ramekins.

Bake until custard is just set. It should still be a bit wiggly in the center, about

Refrigerate until you are ready to serve and for at least 2 hours.

When you are ready to serve them, mix the remaining 2 tablespoons of white sugar with the brown sugar. Remove ramekins from fridge and sprinkle the sugar on top.

If you are adept in the kitchen like Lexy Baker, you can use a kitchen torch to melt the sugar on top of the custard (you'll probably want to use all white sugar for this). Just aim the torch at the sugar-covered top until the sugar is melted and forms a crust. Be careful not to burn it (or set your kitchen on fire).

Leighann Dobbs' husband has banned her from using torches in the kitchen, so she simply puts the ramekins under the broiler for about 2 minutes until the sugar melts.

***

Magic Bars

This is one of my Mom's recipes from the 1970's and I remember it well! So delicious and loaded with calories.

Ingredients:

1 stick butter, melted
1 1/2 cup graham cracker crumbs
6 oz. chocolate bits
1 cup nuts (optional)
1 14 oz. can Eagle sweetened condensed milk
3 1/2 oz. flaked coconut
1 bag mini marshmallows

Preparation:

Preheat oven to 350 degrees (f)

Mix butter and graham crackers and press the mixture firmly into an 8 x 8 pan.

Pour the condensed milk over the crust.

Sprinkle the chocolate bits over the condensed milk.

Sprinkle marshmallows and coconut on top of the bits.

Sprinkle nuts on top.

Bake at 350 degrees (f) for 20 to 30 minutes until browned.

About The Author

USA Today Bestselling author Leighann Dobbs has had a passion for reading since she was old enough to hold a book, but she didn't put pen to paper until much later in life. After a twenty-year career as a software engineer with a few side trips into selling antiques and making jewelry, she realized you can't make a living reading books, so she tried her hand at writing them and discovered she had a passion for that, too! She lives in New Hampshire with her husband, Bruce, their trusty Chihuahua mix, Mojo, and beautiful rescue cat, Kitty.

Find out about her latest books and how to get discounts on them by signing up at:
http://www.leighanndobbs.com/newsletter

If you want to receive a text message alert on your cell phone for new releases, text COZY MYSTERY to 88202 (sorry, this only works for US cell phones!)

Connect with Leighann on Facebook and Twitter
http://facebook.com/leighanndobbsbooks

More Books By Leighann Dobbs:

Mystic Notch
Cats & Magic Cozy Mystery Series

Ghostly Paws
A Spirited Tail
A Mew To A Kill
* * *

Blackmoore Sisters
Cozy Mystery Series

Dead Wrong
Dead & Buried
Dead Tide
Buried Secrets
Deadly Intentions
A Grave Mistake
* * *

Lexy Baker
Cozy Mystery Series

Lexy Baker Cozy Mystery Series Boxed Set Vol 1
(Books 1-4)

Or buy the books separately:

Killer Cupcakes (Book 1)
Dying For Danish (Book 2)
Murder, Money and Marzipan (Book 3)
3 Bodies and a Biscotti (Book 4)
Brownies, Bodies & Bad Guys (Book 5)
Bake, Battle & Roll (Book 6)
Wedded Blintz (Book 7)
Scones, Skulls & Scams (Book 8)
Ice Cream Murder (Book 9)
Mummified Meringues (Book 10)

* * *

Kate Diamond
Adventure/Suspense Series

Hidden Agemda

* * *

Contemporary
Romance

Sweet Escapes
Reluctant Romance
* * *

Dobbs "Fancytales"

Regency Romance Fairytales Series

Something In Red
Snow White and the Seven Rogues
Dancing On Glass
The Beast of Edenmaine
The Reluctant Princess